JUSTIFIABLE VENGEANCE

JUSTIFIABLE VENGEANCE

Lance J. Figgins

Primix Publishing
East Brunswick Office Evolution
1 Tower Center Boulevard, Ste 1510
East Brunswick, NJ 08816
www.primixpublishing.com
Phone: 1-800-538-5788

Published by Primix Publishing: 10/08/2024

ISBN: 979-8-89194-307-0(sc)
ISBN: 979-8-89194-309-4(hc)
ISBN: 979-8-89194-308-7(e)

Library of Congress Control Number: 2024918697

Prologue

Deep in the mountains of south central Colorado, Joe West slipped across a wooded hillside making no more noise than the wind. One soft step at a time, he froze. He was now standing within twenty yards of a huge mule deer buck. The kind of buck every hunter dreamed of, although few ever saw let alone got.

While watching the huge mule deer, he thought as he glanced over his shoulder at his back trail, *Am I ever happy Kay isn't with me. I'd probably be trying to figure out how to get that monster out of here about now.*

He watched as the mountain monarch fed his way across the mountain side and out of sight. With the Buck now gone, Joe carefully started across the mountain side. He was dressed from head to toe in shadow break camouflage, and the lead in a Federal Task Force. They were closing in on what was believed to be a human trafficking drop house.

The intel said there were an estimated twenty to twenty five young people being held, mostly young girls from twelve to sixteen years of age. Now with the activity in the area, authorities figured they had to step it up and move quickly. Members of the task force thought these young people were very possibly being prepared to be sent to Mexico, then on to some of the most terrifying places on earth, places most people had no idea even existed. These places were so dangerous that the life expectancy for an outsider was only a few hours.

The collective future of these young people was nothing short of a life worse than death. They would be forced to have sex with the scum of the earth. The ones who resisted would be beaten, tortured, or forced to use heroin. Within a few short years, death would be their final reward, a death for which they would welcome and pray for.

Pausing, he thought back to what Kay had said as he was preparing to leave. As she hugged and kissed him goodbye, she looked up into his eyes with tears pouring from her's. She pleaded, "Please be careful and bring those soft lips home to me. You have a wife now. A wife that loves and needs you. I know you are good at what you do. My God, Joe. You proved that in the deserts of Arizona last year. I also know that the Taliban and Colombian cartels have placed a million dollar price tag on your life and after what you did in the desert, that number has probably doubled or at least increased."

Pausing, she started to wipe the tears away once again. She reached out and pulled Joe closer and held him a little tighter as she continued, "I know the country needs you. I know that these women, these young people, are in terrible danger. In fact I've stood where they are now and not that long ago. But damn it, Joe, I need you too. Just promise me, please, promise me you'll be extra careful. Hector, Juan and Pablo are all still alive. Now if they are behind this. They'll," she swallowed and wiped her tears away again, looking out the window then back at Joe she continued, "They'll…they'll kill you on sight. Plus, who knows who else you're pissed off and has placed a bounty on you."

Joe held Kay, rocking in place as he stroked her hair. Then pulling her just a little tighter holding her even closer, he reached over and pulled a Kleenex. Carefully, he dabbed at her eyes, wiping the tears away once again as he said, "Adrian asked me to help. I, you, umm, we owe him something we can never repay. We wouldn't be alive today if not for him and the others that came to our rescue. I'll be careful, as careful as I can be." Then smiling slightly, he kissed her and continued, "I promise you'll feel these soft lips kissing you again."

Smiling slightly, Joe looked around before continuing forward one soft step at a time. As he worked his way across the mountain side, he would take one step and stop. Looking at the surroundings, he would take another step and study everything he could see. On his feet he had a pair of white socks covered by a pair of woolen socks, giving him a great feeling of what he was stepping on plus muffling his every step. As he was about to take another step, he froze, something just didn't look right. *What did I miss?* he thought.

As his eyes swept the trail ahead, he saw something. Something that didn't belong in nature. He saw a thin strand of monofilament fishing line. The line was all but invisible although there was a slight reflection in the morning sun.

Standing stone-still, he looked up into the trees for a pendulum swing. Not seeing anything, he carefully scanned the ground for anything out of place. Joe was left handed in a right handed world. With roughly 90% of the population being right handed, the average person would look to the right first and many would forget all about the left side. About four feet to his left, he saw it. There was a grenade. Tied to a tree about two feet above the ground. From where he was standing he could see the line leading to it. The line was nearly invisible if not for the morning sun.

Still searching the area just ahead, he saw a slight rise and a spot where the leaves were not all matted. There were also a few small clumps of black dirt and a rock covered with dirt.

That rock should be clean. It rained here a few days ago. The clumps of dirt should be gone, washed away by that same rain. This hillside had been booby trapped, he thought, *by someone who knew what they were doing.*

Looking around once again, he carefully stepped over the fishing line, not sure if what he saw was real or if they were all hooked together. He continued to look around then ever so slowly he gently dropped to his knees. Taking out his knife, he carefully started probing the area. When his knife touched something metallic, he froze. Carefully, he started removing each leaf one at a time until the area was bare. Working in a half circle, he probed the ground, removing the dirt as he went. He had located an anti-personnel mine. Slowly, ever so carefully, he used his knife like a shovel and continued to remove the surrounding earth and black dirt until he could see the pressure pad. Lowering his head, he saw where the pin would go to make the mine safe to handle. He reached into his pocket and found a nylon tie left over from the previous year's hunting season.

Smiling slightly, he remembered what had happened when Kay had shot her second of two huge Montana bull elk. With a slight chuckle, he carefully slid the nylon tie through the hole. Then taking a small piece of wood, he slipped it behind the nylon tie and slowly tightened it into place.

Taking a deep breath while still on his knees, he wiped the sweat from his forehead. It was a cool crisp day although Joe had sweat running down his face. Taking a second deep settling breath, he stretched and slowly stood and took a few very careful steps. He placed his thumb on the pin and cut the line, removing the line from the grenade and then making sure the pin was all the way in and secured. He placed the grenade in his pack.

Taking out his phone he sent a group text saying: **This hill side is probably full of bombs. I've found two so far, and I'm quite sure there are more. Everyone back out, very carefully, and retreat to the staging point. We can still make this work.**

If I don't blow myself up, he thought.

He continued writing: **I'll move forward. Once I'm in position, I'll send another text. You'll need to come in like the calvary. I'll be at the back door waiting in ambush as all of you come charging in the front.**

Two months later…

Chapter One

Joe West stopped at the end of the driveway. Jumping out, he jogged across the road to get the mail. Getting back into Kay's Yukon Denali, he reached over, dropping the mail into her lap as they headed for the house.

Grabbing several bags of groceries, he followed Kay inside. Putting the bags on the counter as Kay quickly went through the mail. "I'll grab the rest. Anything interesting?" he asked.

As he started walking back towards the garage he heard Kay say, "Nothing much. Just a couple of letters from the state of Montana. Wow, one for each of us." Pausing, she asked, "Joe, did you put in for tags any place other than around here?"

Stopping, Joe replied, "Yep. We are pretty much guaranteed tags around here. Although there are several fantastic areas in Montana to hunt. I've guided in quite a few of them. To be honest I really wouldn't mind drawing a tag or two in most of them. Plus, I always put us in as a party of two. That makes the odds just a tad better. If one of us draws, so does the other."

Kay opened the hunting map of Montana and replied, "It looks like we drew tags south of Missoula all the way down by the Idaho border."

Walking back in, Joe placed the next load of groceries on the counter. Walking up behind Kay and looking over her shoulder, Joe replied, "Wow, really? Down by Soula? I've been in that area several times. Just northeast of there is the winter elk range." Pointing to a spot on the map and continued, "If the weather turns and it starts to snow, we could get into some really great hunting. Plus there would be a very strong possibility of getting a couple of very nice bulls."

Kay smiled and then started to laugh as she replied, "Um, bull? You drew a cow tag." Still looking at the map, she continued, "If this is the area here. Looks like it runs from Soula over towards Wisdom and south to the Idaho border."

"Yes, that's the area," Joe said. A look of astonishment then spread across his face. "What? What do you mean bull? Are you sure?"

Laughing, Kay handed him the paperwork and said, "Read it for yourself. I have a trophy bull tag." With her tag in her hand she pranced and danced off, doing a sexy little shuffle as she sang, "Trophy! Trophy! See right here, it says trophy. And you? Yes you drew a management tag. Yep, you have a management tag." Smiling, she put just a little more wiggle in her step as she flounced across the kitchen to place a tender loving kiss on his lips.

Laughing, Joe glanced back at the paperwork. Looking up and across the kitchen, he continued to laugh as he watched his wife. "We only have one bull tag," he said. "That means we can only shoot one bull. Do you understand? It means that you," pointing at her, he continued, "you can't shoot two bulls. Repeat, you cannot shoot two."

Kay smiled as her eyes produced a seductive look that she knew just melted Joe into a huge puddle of testosterone. She turned around and said, "Okay fine, one bull and one cow. Hey, I'm going to start putting everything away."

Smiling as he walked across the kitchen, Joe wrapped his arms around her and softly kissed her forehead, both cheeks, and the tip of her nose. Then walking back out to her Yukon, he grabbed the last of the bags. As he entered the kitchen he noticed that she had started a pot of coffee. Placing the bags on the counter, he headed for the living room.

It was a cool crisp morning in the mountains of south central Montana. Joe knew that a small fire would help remove the chill from the morning air.

Kay's phone rang. She answered, "Hello," and then froze. The voice was one she would never forget. Dropping the coffee pot, she screamed, "Oh my god! No!"

Joe jumped up and ran for the kitchen. Knocking over an end table, then bouncing off the wall, he found his wife sitting on the floor and crying hysterically. "Kay, what's wrong? Honey, Kay, what's wrong?"

Kay pointed at her phone and said one menacing word, "Hector."

Joe picked up the phone and said, "Hello? Hello? Is anyone there?" The phone was dead. The call had been disconnected. Joe dropped the phone and held Kay. Slowly, he stroked her hair as she tried to tell him what the call was about and what Hector had said.

Chapter Two

Earlier that day.

Colton snapped around and commanded, "I said no. You are to stay home and watch your brother."

Janessa slowly turned as she put her phone to ear and said, "Sorry, Beth. Dad says I can't go." Slowly, she walked down the hall towards her room.

Beth replied, "Wait till they leave and walk over. We can go swimming and you'll be back before they get home."

Janessa thought for a minute, before she replied, "I had better not. Dad would come completely unglued and I'm sure I'd be grounded for life."

Beth replied, "Your dad's bark is far worse than his bite. It won't be that bad. Besides, he likes me and I can smooth it over. If we get caught."

Janessa silently thought for another minute before smiling. She giggled saying,"Okay. See you in a few minutes." Then walking into her room, she put her swimsuit on under her clothes, switched on the television and waited.

Her parents Colton and Desiree were about ready to leave as Colton walked back into the house. Calling to his daughter, he said, "Mom and I will be home in a couple of hours. You stay home and we'll talk when we get back. For now, stay home with your brother."

Coming out of her room. "But Dad," she argued, "Beth and the others are going swimming. Why can't I? I want to go with them now."

Colton stood his ground. "I said stay home." He turned and walked out. Getting in the car, he pointed his finger at the kids who were now standing at the window, watching as their parents left.

Janessa turned and glanced at her brother. She walked towards her bedroom and said, "I'm going to take a nap."

"Yeah, whatever," Tucker answered without looking away from the television.

Five minutes later Janessa slipped out the window and headed for Beth's place. Walking the three blocks, Beth met her at the end of the driveway and together they walked the six blocks to the beach.

Removing their outer clothing, the two girls ran into the lake and swam out to the floating raft. Climbing up the ladder, they stretched out to talk and enjoy the sunshine on the beautiful summer day.

After an hour of sunshine they swam back to shore. Getting dressed, they walked towards home. Talking about boys, school, and that teacher they both disliked, Janessa looked at her phone and said, "I've got to get home. Mom and dad should be there soon."

Janessa started to walk the three blocks home as Beth walked up the driveway towards her home.

A little over a block from home, a car stopped and asked, "Do you know where Jasper Graham lives?"

Janessa looked around as she slowly approached the car. The nice looking young man again asked, "Do you know where Jasper Graham lives?"

Janessa looked up and down the street and said, "I've never heard that name around here."

The man in the car replied, "I have his address here someplace… just a minute and I'll find it." He opened the glove box and started looking around. Picking up a slip of paper, he said, "Here, I think this is it. Yes, here it is. Can you tell me how I can find this address?" he said as he reached over and opened the car door.

As Janessa got closer and closer to the car she was suddenly pushed from behind. The young man placed his hand on the back of her head, forcing her face into his lap as the second guy grabbed both arms and pinned them behind her back. Then forcing her legs together, he put his boots on them as the car drove away.

Lucas Elliot saw what was happening and ran out of his house just as the car started to move. Cutting across his yard and then the neighbor's yard, he came out just twenty feet from where the car had stopped for a stop sign. Then it turned and drove out of sight.

Colton and Desiree arrived home and started unloading the car when Tucker walked out to help. Walking in the house, Desiree called, "Come help me put this stuff away." As she started emptying the bags, Colton and Tucker hauled in the last of the groceries.

Colton said, "Come on, Tucker, there is more in the trunk. You can carry the salt downstairs while I put the other stuff in the storage shed."

As Colton and his son walked out the door, Desiree called again, "Janessa! Hey, Janessa! Get in here."

Colton stopped and said, "Janessa, where are you? Did you hear your mom? Get in here- and I mean now." Turning, he asked Tucker, "Where's your sister?"

Tucker replied, "She should be in her room. She said she was going to take a nap."

Colton stormed down the haul and pushed open the door. He said, "Did you hear us?" Stopping, he looked around and called, "Janessa? Janessa?" Walking back into the living room, he said, "She's not in there." Looking at Tucker, he asked, "Did you see her leave?"

Tucker replied, "No, she said she was going to take a nap. I was watching TV."

Colton looked at his wife and said, "If she goes to Beth's place, she is in a world of trouble and I'm going to ground her for life." Walking outside, he said, "Tucker, unload the car!" Then he walked down the driveway and turned towards Beth's.

Lucas raced back towards his house when he saw Colton calling out, "Colton! Hey, Colton! Lucas ran up breathing hard and said, "I just saw Janessa being forced into a light colored car. I got the license plate and tried to catch it as it left going north."

With his phone to his ear, he listened as the emergency operator said, "9-1-1, what's your emergency?"

Lucas said, "I just saw my neighbor's daughter being forced into a car. Here's my address. Please get an officer here as soon as possible."

The 9-1-1 operator said, "Can you describe the car? Do you have the plate number?"

Lucas said, "It's an off white late model Ford four door with license number 9YT8730. It is going north on 129th street and turned left onto highway 67 and headed out of town just a few minutes ago. Now hurry!"

The 9-1-1 operator repeated the information and said, "I'll have an officer there in five minutes." Lucas heard him post an all-points bulletin over the police radio as he disconnected the call.

Colton and Lucas ran back to the house, stopping just as Desiree walked out. Desiree made eye contact with her husband and asked, "What's wrong? Where is Janessa? What happened?"

He put his arms around her as Lucas started to explain what had happened. As he talked, the tears started flowing and Desiree looked at Colton and said, "No, no. That's not funny. Colton, tell me where my daughter is. You're kidding right?" She started to call out, "Janessa! Janessa! Where are you?"

Just then a police cruiser turned the corner and pulled up to the end of their driveway. The officer got out, walking up, he introduced himself as officer Allen. "Did you report a possible child abduction?" he asked.

Lucas replied, "Possible my ass. I saw the whole thing. The car stopped and one guy said something to get her attention. When she got close enough to the car another came up from behind and pushed her inside and they drove off."

"Don't stand here talking with us!" Desiree yelled. "The car is going east on 67, catch it! My daughter is in that car. Please, go catch it!"

Officer Allen replied, "Calm down, please, calm down. We have every officer in the area looking for that car already. I need you to calm down and tell me everything you can remember. We will find them."

Desiree broke and started crying hysterically pleading, "Why her? Why, why, why?" Looking at Colton, she said, "Why would someone take her? We're not rich. Why?" Looking around, she asked again, "Why?"

Beth was standing at the end of her driveway looking towards Janessa's. Slowly, she started walking when Colton saw her and said, "Beth, have you seen Janessa today or any of your other friends? She was just forced into a car. Are you kids planning some kind of a party? Do you know anything about this?"

Beth looked at Janessa's folks and said, "I don't know anything. I can't believe this happened! And around here!"

As officer Allen took notes, a call came in across the radio. "Dispatch to all cars," it said, "that license is registered to a 2005 silver Chevrolet pickup. Reported stolen yesterday."

Just then another call came through. "Dispatch? I've located the car. It's in a Walmart parking lot. It has that license plate number on it. I need an unmarked car and a plain clothes officer to watch it as soon as possible. If they are in the area I don't want to scare them off. I cannot, repeat, I cannot see the girl from here."

Dispatch replied, "Check the car and continue to patrol the area. We'll have other cars there in a few minutes. To all cars, the child abduction suspect's car has been located in a Walmart parking lot. Officer on scene. Repeat, suspect car located Walmart parking lot. Officer on scene."

Officer Allen looked at Desiree and said, "We have found the car. Now do you have a picture of your daughter?"

Colton opened his wallet and took out a picture of Janessa. Handing it to the officer, he said, "Here is her school picture from last year."

Officer Allen looked at the picture and said, "It's what I expected. She's a very pretty young lady. That's what these pukes look for."

"Just what are you saying?" Colton asked.

Officer Allen looked around before he said, "Traffickers. I'm not saying that's the case here. We don't know yet. It's just a gut feeling. As far as I know. We've never had a abduction like that. Human trafficking is a multi-billion dollar a year business and it's spreading across America at an alarming rate."

Colton looked at his wife standing twenty feet away and said, "Don't mention this to Desiree. For now keep that between us. At least until we know something. I don't want to add to her fears."

While everyone was looking around town and the surrounding area, Officer Allen was still talking with Colten, Lucas, Beth, and Desiree when a call came in from an Officer down in a town 45 miles away. Everyone listened as reports continued to come in.

Chapter Three

Hector and Pedro have been planning this for nearly two months, ever since Joe West had assisted in stopping their business in Colorado.

Two days before, they stole four vehicles and switched all the license plates so none of them had the correct plate and they were different from front to rear. They placed the vehicles in four towns about thirty miles apart where they finally left the last car they would use to get to a small airport where a jet would be meeting them to fly them back to Mexico.

Pulling into Walmart parking lot, Hector took out a knife and said, "If you so much as try and get anyone's attention, I'll slide this between your ribs and you'll die a very slow and painful death right here in this parking lot and no one will see you!"

Carefully, Hector and Pedro switched cars and headed back west on 67 into town and out the west side. It was thirty miles to where they had another stolen car waiting for them.

As they left the parking lot, Janessa started to struggle. She was trying to fight a battle she couldn't win. Hector slapped her several times and then punched her in the kidneys. Janessa quit fighting and laid there with tears running down her cheeks.

Driving through town, they met several cops' lights flashing heading east on 67. Pedro watched in the mirror as he proceeded west out of town.

Hector looked at Pedro and said, "This is going to be so good. I'll finally have what I want and there's not a thing Joe West or anyone else can do about it."

Twenty minutes later, they arrived at a Home Depot. Getting out of the car, they casually walked to a stolen Jeep Cherokee. Leaving the parking lot, then turned north as they took highway 305 north 20 miles to Des Moines where they had yet another stolen vehicle waiting for them in a mall parking lot.

Hector watched as they met two state patrol cars. Glancing in the mirror, he said, "Watch your driving. I don't think they have figured anything out yet, but it won't take them long to put it all together. It's just under thirty miles to the next town and from there we will switch one last time and head north. I'm going to call the plane so they are waiting at the airport when we arrive. Once we are airborne it'll be just a few hours and we'll be in Mexico. Then I can call the West family. I know Kay will trade herself for her granddaughter. I'll have Kay. The cartels can have Joe. And we can sell this pretty little sweet thing," he slapped her back side, "for a tidy little profit to boot."

Pedro looked over at Janessa, her hard firm muscled body and asked, "Can I have the girl when we get back to Mexico?"

Janessa's eyes snapped open as she started to struggle again. Hector slapped her hard on the side of the face and said, "Not yet, I need her perfectly healthy until after I contact Joe and Kay West. After that I don't care what you do."

Ten miles from the airport they met a state patrol. Pedro watched as the car slowed and turned around. Hector slid a .45 out from under his coat. Working the action, he ensured it was loaded and laid it in his lap.

One mile from the airport and the trooper turned on the lights. Pedro signaled and pulled to the side. Hector picked up the pistol and slid a newspaper over it. As the officer approached the passenger side of the car, Hector lifted his hand and fired one shot into his chest. Lifting the officer off his feet and knocking him over backwards, he tumbled onto the side of the road and down into the ditch.

Quickly, Pedro stepped on the gas and a minute later they turned into the airport, driving around the fence and right up to the waiting jet. In a matter of seconds all three were in the jet and the pilot pushed the throttles forward as they taxied to the active runway. Hector told the pilot, "Get this thing in the air now. Do whatever you need while we taxi. So you can get this thing airborne faster."

As they approached the runway, the pilot radioed local traffic. Not slowing, he continued out onto the runway. Pushing the throttles full forward, less than thirty seconds later the nose lifted and the corporate jet climbed skyward and banked southwest and headed for the deserts of Mexico.

Officer Bill Oliver slowly got to his knees then to his feet. His radio had been crushed when he landed on it. Slowly, he made his way to his cruiser. Picking up the mic, he called dispatch and reported the shooting. He asked, "Do you have any information on the car I pulled over?"

Dispatch answered, "The Chevrolet was reported stolen yesterday morning. It seems that four vehicles have been stolen in the last twenty four hours. We have located three. I have an ambulance en route to your location. Stay put, he'll be there in ten minutes."

State patrol Bill Oliver replied, "I'm about a mile from Williams airport. I'm headed there now. I'll radio in from there. Requesting backup now. Repeat, Williams airport requesting backup."

A call went out across the radio "State Patrol requesting backup. Williams airport, all units, State Patrol requesting backup, Williams airport."

As the police in the area started reporting their location and who was en route to the Williams airport, Officer Oliver called in, "I believe I have found the fourth car. It's at the Williams airport." Going around the fence, lights and sirens went off as he raced towards the runway. He watched as a small corporate size jet lifted off and passed directly over him. It banked southwest and disappeared from sight.

Chapter Four

Desiree looked at Colton and said, "My God, what are we going to do? Why is this happening?"

Colton replied, "I don't know babe. Although the first thing tomorrow morning I'll call the bank and see how much we can get. Hopefully that idiot is wrong and this isn't what they are saying. We need to see how much money we can get to pay the ransom when they call."

A few minutes later the Chief of Police Dylan Meyers arrived to talk with and give advice to Desiree and Colton. He had already contacted the FBI. This was their case as soon as the suspects had fled in an airplane. They were sure they would cross state lines and possibly international borders as well.

Late that afternoon, FBI agent Dale Mowers got out of his car. Walking up along with Dylan Smith, he introduced him to everyone while the other agents started setting up equipment.

Dale then started asking questions. Lucas told his story again while Dale started taking notes. Then they started talking with officer Allen and state patrol officer Bill Oliver. Soon the story started coming together. Bill looked at Mowers and said, "These guys, these suspects, looked to be possibly Mexican."

Without looking around, Agent Mowers replied, "This could be a sex trafficking ring." Desiree stood only a few feet away, heard this and started crying again as she said, "Sex trafficking? What do you mean sex trafficking?"

Colton grabbed his wife and stood there trying to comfort her as he glared at Mowers. Turning, he walked her back into the kitchen where he calmly got her sitting with a couple of the neighbor ladies that had stopped over for support and to try and help where and when they could.

Colton walked back into the living room and said to Dylan, "Tell that FBI dude to be more careful. Things like what he just said don't need to be said in front of my wife. For god's sake, it's our daughter he's talking about."

Dale overheard the conversation and replied, "We need you to face the facts."

Colton asked, "Just which facts are you talking about?"

Dale replied, "She's young and pretty. That is exactly what these guys are looking for."

Desiree walked back in and told Colton, "I'm going to call mom. I need to talk to her. I sure wish she and Joe lived closer."

"Where do they live?" Dale asked.

Colton replied, "They just built a new home in Montana. Southwest of Billings."

Dale asked, "By any chance are you talking about Joe and Kay West?"

With an utterly shocked look on her face, Desiree replied, "Yes. Do you know them?"

Dale swore under his breath and replied, "Yes- I do! I don't want that, that trouble-causing ass around here."

Looking at agent Aaron Thomas then back at Colton, he said, "I'm going to leave two guys here to watch over you and the equipment we've set up. I'll be back tomorrow morning. Hopefully by then we will have been in contact and can see what their demands are." Then he continued, "Aaron, you come with me.

As they walked away, Aaron said, "You must have had trouble with this Joe West. What happened?"

Mowers replied, "Yeah. He's the reason I'm now stationed here in dip shit Iowa rather than the Hover building in DC. He's the worst kind of a gun toting, redneck, vigilante asshole you'll ever find. Him and that damn cowboy Logan Lathrop."

Chapter Five

Still sitting on the kitchen floor, Joe continued to hold Kay. Softly, he stroked her hair while saying, "Calm down. I'm right here. Just calm down and tell me what he said."

Kay looked up and said, "Oh my god, Joe. He said he has Janessa. I have to call Desiree. Joe he- he-" she stuttered, "he has my granddaughter."

Just as she said those words, the phone beeped. Joe grabbed the phone and in a voice that sounded like he was about to kill someone, he answered, "HELLO?!"

Desiree answered, "Umm, Joe, is that you?"

Joe shook his head and answered, "Umm, yes, Desiree. Your mom, umm your, your mom is right here. Just a second."

With that he pushed the speaker to Kay. "Hi Des," she said. Looking at Joe, she continued, "How are you doing?"

Desiree broke down and started crying. "Mom, mom, someone- umm- something has happened. It looks like Janessa has been taken. The FBI is here now. Oh mom, what am I going to do? Mom, someone took Janessa."

"Des, Des, please calm down. I will be there tomorrow. It'll take a few hours to get everything ready and we'll leave before daylight. We can be there in about six hours, maybe less if we have a tail wind."

"Oh, that would be great. Mom, I need you," she responded.

Kay said, "We'll see you tomorrow. Joe and I have some money put away. We'll give you whatever you need or they want. We'll get her back." With that, she disconnected. Looking at Joe, she said, "You know what he wants. He wants me and Pablo wants you. It's going to be bad isn't it?"

Joe smiled. "Nope. They can have me. I'll go, I'll do anything to get Janessa back."

Getting up, Joe walked into his gun room. Flipping a switch on the wall, he walked to the last shelf and pushed. As it opened, he flipped a light switch on. Looking at the wall, he picked up two M16s plus several bandoliers of ammunition. Then looking at the pistols, he grabbed two .357 and two 1911 H and K .45. Walking across, he opened the safe. Grabbing a small backpack, he loaded flash bang grenades, fragmentation grenades, and smoke and teargas grenades, plus several boxes of ammunition. Closing everything up, he walked back into the living room. He knew it was going to be bad and probably very bloody. He had done everything he could do to keep his senses up and to keep his woodsmen skills sharp. He was in really good physical shape. Although he was still good enough to survive. To outfox the fox.

Looking up, he said quietly, "I'll do what I have to do to keep her safe and away from Hector."

Turning, he watched as Kay walked into the room. Putting her arms around him, she said, "I'm going to do what he says. If that means I have to go with him, then I don't want you to try and stop me. If he tells you to stay away, that's what I want. Joe, you can't save us both. So please just save her."

Joe looked into the eyes of the women he had promised to love, honor, obey, and protect. In this case he could not both obey and protect. Kay knew that and so did he. Thinking, he said, "Kay, honey. I'll do as you say until I have a choice to protect you or obey you. Then I'm going to protect first. I'm going to get Janessa back alive and unharmed. I'm going to kill whoever gets in my way. Des thinks we are going to be there in the morning. We are going to be there tonight. You are going to her house. I'm going hunting. I'll get all the information I can from the agency. Then screw that border and the authorities. I'm going to Mexico and all the way to Columbia if I have to. They won't hurt her until we don't comply with their demands. I'll talk to the FBI agent and make sure they comply. I have to call Logan and have him watch the house and take care of the horses." Turning, he picked up his phone, pushed Logan's number and walked away.

Logan answered on the first ring and said, "So tell me. Have you found a new pickup yet?"

Joe replied, "Yep. I'll have a new GMC here in a few days. Hey, buddy. Kay and I are going to fly to Iowa for a week or so. She wants to see her kids and grandkids. Can you take care of the horses and watch the house for us?"

"Absolutely," answered Logan, "Anything wrong?"

"Nope," Joe lied, "Just going to visit family. After what happened in Arizona last winter, she wants to see everyone again. If we get out of here quick enough, we can be there in five or six hours. I've already looked at the radar and it's clear. All I have to do is get over the eastern range and it's pretty much clear flying."

Logan replied, "Don't worry about a thing. Stay in touch and have a great time."

Disconnecting the call, Logan looked at Rene and said, "I know Joe's voice. Something's wrong. Call Kay and see if you can find out."

Joe walked up the steps to his office. He opened the bottom drawer of his desk and started moving things around until he found a small box. Opening the box, he picked up his badge that read DEA/ Border Protection identification and placed a call to Smithfield Va. As the operator answered, he asked for the personnel department. The phone rang a few times, then a lady answered, "Personnel, can I help you?"

Joe replied, "Yes, this is Captain Randy Jackson. I need to speak with the Reinstatement Department."

The operator hit a few keys and said, "Yes, sir. Just a minute please." Thirty seconds later, Steve Swenson answered saying, "Is this some kind of a joke? Who is this?"

Joe laughed and said, "No joke Steve, this is Randy. Although my name is Joe now. Please use that whenever you are talking to me. Although use Randy when you have to. Although please never at the same time while trying to identify me. Now listen." Pausing, he took a deep breath and continued, "You need to reinstate me like now. I need every clearance you can get me. Plus make sure I get my K-1 clearance as well. My granddaughter has been kidnapped by my old friends in Columbia. I need a secure satellite phone sent to an address in Iowa. I'll email you the address in a few minutes."

Steve said, "Iowa? Anywhere near Cherokee, Iowa?"

"Yes, why?" Joe replied.

"I heard about a kidnapping in Cherokee just an hour or so ago. I was told there's an FBI agent already there."

"Perfect," replied Joe. "By any chance do you know who's there? Although more importantly, can I trust him or her?"

"Just a minute," Steve replied. "Let me check on who it is. It says here that an agent by the name of Dale Mowers is in charge. Oh hey, wait. Here's an eyes-only bulletin. Umm, Joe be careful. The agency thinks he might be dirty."

Joe sat there thinking before he answered, "Oh, boy. I already had a run in with him. I kicked his ass when he was in charge of the human trafficking investigation here in Montana a year or so ago. Don't send the satellite phone to him. Send it to the address I sent you a few minutes ago. I'll keep you posted."

Steve took a deep breath and said, "I think I know what you are planning. I've read every report connected to you in every way. All I can say is be careful and, yes, please keep me posted. I'll do everything I can to help you. Oh, and by the way. You'll have to get the K-1 clearance from Oliver Scott."

Joe let out a long slow breath as he replied, "Oliver Scott, why him? He's an idiot and we've had several disagreements. I turned his stupid ass in when he nearly blew my cover in Columbia. No one was supposed to mention me. That dumb ass gave my real name to an informant that was working both sides."

"K-1 is something we just don't hand out that often anymore and Homeland Security," Steve added, "is where you'll have to try and get it."

Joe sat there thinking when he said, "This is going to be out of country. Can I get one through Langley?"

Steve made a few keystrokes before he said, "That's worse. There you'll need to talk with Chip Jacobs. Do you remember him? He's the guy that sent the team of Seals after you. Trying to kill you before we could bring you out. I think that he acted totally on his own. Trying to make a name for himself. Someone at Langley intercepted a message and contacted the team to call them off. That would have been the shit storm of the century if you would have killed any of them."

Joe thought for a minute before he said, "Oh my god, yes it sure would have been. I guess I'll try Olly first. Listen if I can't get it. Can you think of anyone else that might go over their heads and help me. I'm going with or without it and I'll be the most wanted man in Columbia on both sides."

"I'll see who I can talk with. Um, Joe if you don't get it. We now have an extradition treaty with the Colombian government. I don't think we'll be able to help you. You'll also be wanted in the US. So be extra careful."

"Hey, I'll catch up with you tomorrow," Joe replied, "and see what you can find out." Breaking the call, Joe started looking through his private equipment as Kay's phone rang.

She quickly blew her nose before answering and said in a voice as cheerful as possible, "Hi Rene, what are you up to?" Trying to make sure they don't talk about her.

"Joe just asked Logan to take care of the horses and watch the house," Rene replied. "Is there anything else you need? Logan said Joe didn't sound right. Like something might be wrong."

Joe stood up and put everything in two cases. Walking into the living room, he stood for a minute and listened before he whispered, "I'm going to check over the plane and put this in it." He held up the two cases.

Kay nodded her head as she replied, "Oh, Rene, just family stuff. My daughter and son-in-law are having some problems. Joe and I should just stay home. Although she asked us to come. You know how it is. You do everything you can to make your family happy. So we are going to fly there tomorrow and spend a few days there. We should be back by the end of the week."

"Oh okay," Rene responded, "if you need anything, please let us know."

Disconnecting the call, Rene looked at Logan and said, "Yeah something is definitely wrong. I could hear her voice shaking. I'm not sure what it is but she's scared. I think we should be ready to go on a minute's notice."

Logan grabbed his notebook and after checking the numbers, he said, "The spring roundup is nearly done. We have what I want to ship now in one pasture. Plus what I'm going to ship later in another. I've already negotiated the first contract and called the trucking companies. Jesse and Jerod can actually finish this if we have to go. So yeah, let's get about three quarters ready so we can load up and go if we get a call."

Looking out the window, Logan said, "Wow, looks like Joe is at the hanger now. I think I'll drive down there and check on him."

Joe watched out the window as Logan drove towards the hanger. Quickly, he got the two cases into the nose storage compartment and the hatch closed and locked just before Logan walked in saying, "Hey, buddy. Is there anything else you want to do?"

Spinning around and acting like he was surprised to see Logan there, he said, "Damn dude, you scared the shit out of me."

Logan started to laugh and said, "Sorry, I really didn't mean to do that."

Joe took a deep breath like he was trying to settle down before he replied, "After Arizona I guess I'm still a little jumpy."

Logan shook his head as he said, "Yeah, I nearly punched Jesse a few days after we got home. When he walked up behind me. Anyway, when are you leaving?"

Joe replied, "Kay's packing a couple of suitcases now. If I can get over the east range I'll climb to say 12,000 and head east. We just need to get going soon. I want to be in the air and over the range before dark. Or we won't leave until morning. I really don't want to have to fly a route out of here and stay on it until I'm over 13,000 to stay clear of the rocks. Even with Billings control vectoring me."

Logan looked at his friend and said, "Okay, what's going on Joe? Level with me."

Joe replied, "I can't Logan, not right now. Although if it gets as bad as I think it's going to I'll call. I'll be sending Kay back here and I'll meet you somewhere. We'll be going hunting. In Columbia."

Logan looked around before saying, "I'll be ready." Grabbing his best friend's hand, he continued, "I'll be ready. We need to finish what started a few years ago. One way or another we need to finish it."

Looking at Logan, Joe said, "Yeah. They all need to die."

Joe and Logan were still talking when the door opened and Kay walked in with two suitcases. Handing them to Joe, she said, "I did a walk through of the house. Everything is locked and closed. I think we are ready to go."

Putting just a little emphasis on everything, Logan knew what she meant. She had been in Joe's private gun room. The room that was actually hidden behind an electric locking system with more military hardware that most people have never heard of, let alone seen.

Joe put the suitcases into the back seat. Getting in the pilot seat, he flipped the switch for the fuel pumps. Watching as the pressure climbed, he pushed the button to start the first engine. Still watching the pressure, he started the second one. Giving them a few minutes, Logan opened the hanger door and Joe taxied out into the Montana evening. Switching off the passenger side engine, Kay gave Logan a hug as he closed the door and together they walked to the plane. Kay stepped on the wing as Joe pushed her door open. Turning, he saw Logan standing on the pilot's side behind the wing. Joe opened his door, shaking his friend's hand and he said," I'll talk to you in a few days."

Logan replied, "We'll be ready."

Joe pushed the button to restart the right engine. Checking the gauges, he pushed the throttles forward and headed for the runway. As he lined up the runway, Kay's phone rang. She turned the phone towards Joe. Taking a quick glance, he said, "Don't answer it. He'll call back and that'll give us a few minutes to climb out and open the flight plan. Then I can put it on the plane's headsets and we can both listen."

Kay let the call go to voicemail as they gained speed and lifted off. In a straight out full power climb, Joe flipped a few switches contacting air traffic control and opened the fight plan. Then contacting Billings control he got a vector and banked to the east. Just as they passed through one and two thousand feet Kay's phone rings again. Joe flipped a switch.

"Hello?"

Hector's voice came through their headsets as he said, "I have your granddaughter. The only way she won't be sold is if you agree to take her place. Otherwise I'll sell her and she'll be someone's little whore."

Joe quickly sent a pre-typed text to Steve: **This is the call I told you about. Try and trace it.**

Then taking her phone and punching in a number, he hit the phone. Steve didn't say a word, he just patched the call to the computer geek next to him. This all took a few seconds as Hector said, "So, do I have your attention? The only way she'll survive this is by you coming to me. Plus, I don't want to see Joe anywhere in the area."

Kay replied, "Yes, we have a deal but I want you to send me pictures of her every day. I'll send you what I want the picture to look like or what I want her to be doing. The first time you miss the picture you won't ever see me again. Although I'm quite sure Joe will see you."

"I'm not playing any games," Hector said. "I want you, not this brat. Although I'm quite sure I can find a lot of men that would love her. So remember, only you. I don't want to see Joe."

Kay looked at Joe and said, "I promise you won't see Joe. When are you going to contact me again? Oh, and send me a picture of her holding a sign that says 'Hi grandma.' I'll wait for the picture now. I want to see for myself that she's alive."

Hector swore. "You'll have it in a few minutes."

Kay looked at Joe and mouthed the words, *I'm trying to keep him on the phone.* Then out loud so Hector could hear, "I'm waiting right here and now. I'll do what you want and listen to you. But I want that picture. Plus, I want to talk to her."

"Hang on while I find a pen and paper," Hector said.

Looking at Joe, she whispered, "I'm trying to keep him on the phone. I saw your text."

Joe smiled as he sent another text: **Do you have a location yet?**

Stevens' answer came before Joe could put the phone down: **Yes, they are in Columbia.**

Joe shook his head and replied, **I was afraid of that.**

Hector came back on the line and said, "I just sent you the picture you asked for. I'll contact you tomorrow with more instructions." He disconnected the call before Kay could reply.

Joe dialed Steve's number and he answered on the first ring. "Yes, we got his location. He was bouncing off of three towers so it should be within say twenty feet."

"Perfect," Joe replied, "I'll talk to you tomorrow after we talk to the kids. Although I'm not telling the FBI anything. I'm only going to be there until we talk to Hector. As soon as he gives her instructions I'll be on the first plane to where she is going. I want to be there ahead of time to look around."

Disconnecting the call, he looked at Kay and said, "I'm afraid this is going to be bad. It's also probably going to get really bloody. Although I swear before god I'll get her back. And I'll kill anyone that gets in my way."

Kay looked at Joe. This was a Joe she didn't know. It was not the man she fell in love with. This man sitting next to her was nothing less than a highly trained professional killer.
Kay slowly slid her hand across and put it on Joe's leg. She felt the anger slowly disappear from his body and he became the loving man she married. She could feel it as he slowly became her husband once again.

Joe reached across the plane and gave Kay a quick kiss. He said, "I'm afraid you might see a part of me you've never seen before nor did I ever expect you to see. It's a cold-blooded killer named Randy Jackson who was trained in the military by the best of the best. In order to get Janessa back, that man had to come back to the surface. I've done everything I can to keep him buried deep inside."

Kay looked at her husband. Then thinking for a minute, she said, "I don't care who you become, or what you have to do. Just get her back."

Joe looked straight forward for a couple of seconds before shifting his gaze onto the instruments and gauges on the plane. Trimming the plane for level flight, he picked up his phone. Pressing a number, he flipped a few switches before turning to Kay and saying, "I need to ask a few questions. So please let me talk until I get what I need then you can."

As the call connected, Kay heard Colton's voice. Starting to say something, Joe put his finger across his lips and said, "Colton, are you alone? If not, walk away from everyone before saying anything."

A few seconds later, Colton replied, "I'm alone now. Where are you and when will you be here? This FBI asshole is scaring us. He keeps saying we might never see her again."

Looking at Kay, he saw the tears starting to run down her cheeks. Flipping a switch, he isolated himself with Colton and said, "I'll do everything I can to help get her home safe and sound. Kay and I know who has her, what this is all and now I have a very good idea of where they are. I'll answer all of your questions later. For right now you just have to trust me. Sometime later today or tomorrow a package is going to arrive in my name. Make sure you get it and don't give it to anyone. We will be there in a few hours. Can you pick us up at the airport? Say in." Taking a

quick glance at the GPS airspeed and ground speed he continues,
"Say, three hours?"

Colton replied, "Absolutely. There are so damn many people around here now. No one would even realize I'm gone. Damn it Joe, now you are scaring me."

Joe replied, "I'll fill you in when we get there. Now listen, here's Kay."

Flipping a switch that brought Kay back into the conversation, Colton said, "Kay, Kay I heard about you from a guy named Hector. I had Desiree's phone. He said he wanted to trade Janessa for you. I didn't tell anyone about the call. I wanted to call you but I couldn't get away from everyone. Kay, what's going on?"

Looking at Joe, Kay replied, "Yes, we got the same call. I talked to Janessa for just a few seconds. She's okay and Joe and I have agreed to the trade."

Colton said, "That Hector asshole said he didn't want to see Joe anywhere near where the trade is to take place."

Joe broke in and said, "I promised him that he wouldn't see me. I already told him that. This is a simple trade, although once Janessa is safe all bets are off."

Entertaining the airport traffic area, Joe came in a little hot and floated a long way down the runway before simply forcing the plane to land. Stopping at the gas pumps, he told the fuel attendant to fill all the tanks including the belly tank. After tying the plane down, he joined Colton and Kay inside. Looking at his son-in-law, he said, "Please just tell me what he said. Don't add, don't subtract."

"He told me he had Janessa and wants to trade her for Kay," Colton replied. "He also said that if he sees you anywhere he'll kill them both." Colton looked from Joe to Kay and back as he said, "My god Joe, why would he say that? What the hell does he want and who is he?"

"He's a slime ball scum of the earth, a human trafficking ass. He wants Kay and so do I. So far I've been able to stay a step ahead of him. With just a little luck I still am. Now come on, let's go to your house. I need to listen to everyone and everything so I can get all the information and start forming some kind of a plan." *Please, god, help me. I need to save them both,* Joe thought to himself.

As they walked out of the airport terminal Colton asked, "Joe, who are you? I overheard that FBI agent. He doesn't like you or Kay."

Joe smiled as he said, "It'll be okay. I'll let him think he's in charge. As soon as Hector contacts Kay again I'm gone. That'll make him happy and take some of the pressure off. Kay will make the deal to meet, only I'll be there ahead of time. With a little luck I'll get Janessa before the trade takes place. Then I'll get her to safety, find Kay, and bring her home also."

Colton looked at Kay and then at Joe as he said, "What makes you so sure? Plus, how can you do that? You are only one man."

Looking straight forward, Joe simply said, "I can and I will." Then looking at Colton, he continued, "That's a promise." Glancing at Kay, Joe then turned and looked out the window.

Colton glanced at Kay then focused back on the road as he drove back towards his house-Desiree and the nightmare was unfolding in front of them. Kay looked over at Joe who was still looking out the window. The transformation had begun. The man she loved was changing right before her eyes. She could see the change and understood what he really was. Kay said a silent prayer that he would change back into the man she loved.

Arriving back at the house, Colton parked on the street and together all three headed for the driveway with Joe a step behind. Always the hunter, he carefully scanned the surroundings, moving his eyes from quadrant to quadrant using his off center vision. A slight smile came to his face as he realized what he was doing without even thinking about it. After years of survival depending on no one but himself, his skills were naturally coming back to the surface. Colton opened the door as the three of them walked inside.

Desiree saw her mother and ran to her. The tears started instantly as mother and daughter stood holding each other. Des started talking a hundred miles an hour. Through the tears and sobs, Joe heard everything he needed. As the two FBI agents walked up, Dean Pascal held up his badge and said, "We need some identification."

Joe handed them his license and said, "I'm Joe West, that lady is my wife Kay. I'll get her license in a couple of minutes."

Dean put his badge away and held Joe's license in one hand. He said, "We were told you are not allowed to be here. In fact, you're not even allowed on the property."

Joe looked at the two agents. Making a slight change in his stance, he said, "I'm staying and I don't believe you two are enough to make me leave. Although you are more than welcome to try."

Dean watched as Joe changed the way he was standing. Recognizing the stance, he knew instantly he was looking at a highly trained combat operative, a professional killer. Touching Frank's arm, he said, "We can deal with this tomorrow. He's Dale's problem, not ours." They both turned and went back to their posts.

Desiree broke away from her mother and hugged Joe. Turning to Colton, she said, "While you were gone we got a delivery. I put it on the counter. Here, it says it's for you." Opening the small package part way, he handed it to Joe who turned away to finish opening it. Sliding the secure satellite phone in his pocket, he turned back and put his arm around Kay.

Across the room, Frank watched as Joe slipped the phone away and said, "West got a package we missed. Maybe we should take it away and keep it until morning and give it to Mowers."

Dean replied, "Go ahead. Be my guest. Although you had better call an ambulance before you try. Make sure they have a life flight bird on stand by. You'll be needing it. I watched him. He's not a run of the mill idiot like Mowers says. There's something about him that says training and a lot of it. Me? I'm staying clear of him. He's Mower's problem, not ours and definitely not mine."

Colton asked, "You are staying here tonight, right?"

Kay glanced at Joe as he nodded before saying, "Yes, of course. As long as you have room for us."

Desiree said, "Of course we have room. There's always room for you." She started to cry. "You can stay in Janessas room."

Joe looked around and said, "I think we had better stay in your extra bedroom downstairs. I'm sure the FBI wants to look through her room again. Maybe many more times. The smallest thing could become very important later." Glancing at the two agents, Joe picked up the suitcases and headed for the downstairs bedroom. Putting everything away, he turned as Kay walked in and said, "Colton just gave Desiree a sleeping pill. The doctor told him she would get a little goofy but they should put her out. The two FBI guys are at their posts and I think I need to get some sleep. I'm completely done in."

Joe walked out. Going upstairs, he looked around double checking the doors before heading back to Kay.

Closing the bedroom door, he stood there listening for a minute before slowly opening it again. Listening ever so closely, he heard the slightest squeak as the door passed through the quarter way open position. Closing it again, he turned to see Kay staring at him. Smiling, he said, "Just making sure."

His transformation was complete. Laying next to Kay with his arm around her, he was barely asleep. He could hear Kay breathing and the agents as they walked from post to post checking the house. He heard the stairs as someone went up or down. He heard the slight squeak of the bedroom door as it opened past the quarter way point. Rolling onto his back, he could see the red anti-glare light as it flashed through the room. He watched as
Frank moved through the room looking for whatever Joe had received. With his right hand controlling the anti-glare light, Frank's left hand moved towards the nightstand and the phone laying there. Joe's left arm flashed, grabbing Frank's left arm and bending it backwards at the wrist in a second. Joe's right hand was wrapped around his left and he was forcing his wrist past

its natural position. Twisting the arm around and in, bringing it up behind his back, and nearly dislocating his shoulder, he cried out in pain. Joe wrapped his left arm across Frank's throat and forced him out of the room and up the stairs.

Giving him a push, he said, "I'm not going to say this again. You two are not enough to remove me. Don't try again or someone's going to get hurt. This is your only warning. If you try again I'll break your arm or worse. Stay away and leave us alone. Simply do your job and protect the family here."

Turning, he walked back downstairs to a wide awake Kay who exclaimed, "What the hell just happened?"

"Frank wanted the phone I got this evening," Joe replied. "It's a secure satellite phone from some old friends. Tomorrow I'll be spending most of my time outside talking with them. Once you hear from the asshole I'll be gone, although I'll program a few names and numbers into your phone for emergencies."

Tears started to slip from Kay's eyes as she asked, "Can you get her back? Is there any chance you can also find me and bring me back also?"

Joe took three quick steps, wrapping his arms around her. He kissed her forehead and said, "I'll bring you both back or I'll die in Columbia. That's a promise." While still holding her, he continued, "When Hector calls tomorrow I'm going to suggest trading me for her. I'm worth at least a million dollars. Maybe he's money hungry enough to do that. I'll try and convince him that with me in the hands of the cartels he would only have to deal with Logan to get you and Rene."

Kay stepped back and exclaimed, "No! Absolutely not. I know that they would torture and kill you. You wouldn't have a chance. No, no, no. That is *not* going to happen!"

Joe looked into Kay's eyes. "I'll find you and bring you home also. I've talked to Springfield. I'm being restated as an agent. I'll have the DEA backing me. I'm keeping my rank and getting all of my clearances."

Kay looked at him with a puzzled look and asked, "I overheard you say something about a K-1 clearance? What is that?"

"Honey," Joe replied, "right now you don't need to know about that. I wish you hadn't heard me talking about it."

Kay stood there for a minute. Then looking at him again, she said, "It's a clearance to kill, isn't it?"

Joe stood there trying to decide how to answer her and said, "Yes, it is. I was licensed by the federal government to kill. Although I was told who I could kill and when. This time I need an open K-1 which means I can kill anyone that has anything to do with her kidnapping. I don't think I'll get it. It's not going to stop me. It just means when this is over I could possibly be arrested and brought up on murder charges."

Joe got dressed and walked upstairs. He made a pot of coffee. Looking over at Frank, he asked, "How's your wrist? You're lucky I didn't break your arm or your damn fool neck."

Frank stared at him and said, "It'll be alright, although when Mowers gets here, if I was you I'd be gone. We have to report this to him and he's going to be some kind of pissed."

Joe looked at Frank and replied, "He doesn't bother me in the slightest. He's nothing but a blowhard idiot. Oh, and it's better to be pissed off than pissed on. If he causes any trouble I'll simply kick his ass again. This time all the way back to the Hoover building and they can deal with him there."

Frank looked across the room and said, "You say that now. It'll be different when there are more than just us two here. You won't act so big and tough then."

Stopping at the top of the stairs, Joe turned and said, "You had better hope it doesn't come to that. You won't be alive in the end." Walking down the steps, he met Kay fully dressed and with her head up. Turning, Joe followed her out onto the deck to enjoy their coffee and a clear cool Iowa morning.

Chapter Six

Joe's satellite phone rang. Pushing the button, Joe answered, "It's morning and I hope you have good news."

Steve replied, "You are still a smart ass. Listen, I've got your clearance. Although they want you to go through proper channels first. As a last resort you'll be going in as Commander Randy Jackson. Your cover is that you are looking for a terrorist wanted by the federal government."

"Perfect," Joe replied. "I'll call Ollie and see what that idiot has to say. I'll get back to you in an hour or so." Disconnecting, he looked at Kay and said, "It's a go. One way or another it's a go. I need to make a few calls. Please be quiet and head off anyone that heads this way."

Dialing a number, he waited as the phone rang. A man answered by saying, "Oliver Scott, how can I help you?"

"Hi Oliver, this is Randy Jackson," Joe replied. "I need my K-1 clearance. Only this time I need to be open."

"Who is this? Randy Jackson is dead."

"I'm sorry to disappoint you and burst your bubble but sorry you missed. I'm very much alive and I was told I had to get my clearance from you." Continuing as sarcastically as possible, he said, "So you either give me the clearance or I'll go over your head. That way you can remain the same no account idiot you always have been."

Just as Oliver was reaching to hang up, Joe said, "Don't hang up on me. Call your boss on the other line and check. Or simply push a few keys on the computer in front of you and you can see I've been reinstated and active. I've got a mission coming up and I need that clearance."

"Well you won't get it from me," Oliver replied. "I hope you screw up and I get to testify against you."

"Either sign the clearance or I'll be in your office soon. I'll start breaking bones until you do. Now be the nice puppet you are and sign the damn thing before I get pissed and walk upstairs now and break your damn jaw!"

Oliver started to shake. "You're here!? In Springfield!? Now!?"

Joe smiled as he said, "Yes, Ollie. I'm downstairs. I was going to walk in and get it. Although I'm not completely sure I could stop myself from breaking your damn jaw when you started shooting your mouth off so I figured I'd call and give you a chance first."

"I'm going to call security and make sure they keep you out of the building. Then I'm going to file a complaint against you." He hung up the phone.

Joe laughed as he said, "Well, that didn't take long. I've got to call Steve. It looks like I'm about to become Commander Randy Jackson again."

Dialing Steve's number and waiting, Steve answered on the second ring and said, "You trouble-causing sarcastic prick. That idiot came flying into my office and said you were in the building and I had to get him a body guard. That you were going to break his jaw if he didn't give you an open K-1. My god, you've only been active for two days and I'm already cleaning up after you." He paused while he listened to Joe laughing on the other end. "Damn it, Randy, now listen. Call General Jacobson. He's going to sign your clearance. He's already been briefed and knows the story. I think he knows you. I believe he may have been at Bragg during your training."

At seven in the morning, Dale Mowers along with two other agents walked in to relieve the guys from the night shift.

Frank walked up and said, "We've got bad news. West and his wife are here. They arrived yesterday evening. Also, West got a package yesterday. We didn't see the delivery guy, although I think it's a phone. He damn near broke my arm last night when I tried to get it."

Mowers looked through the window to see Joe and Kay drinking coffee and talking. Turning back, he snapped, "I told you two to keep your damn eyes open. I needed to know everything that happens. You should have demanded that he turn it over. Damnit, do I have to do everything?"

Dean replied, "Hey, if you want it that bad, you go and demand he gives it to you. I really would enjoy watching."

With a dirty look on his face, Mowers turned and walked outside. Pressing a couple of buttons, he waited for the call to connect and said, "We have a problem. Joe West is here. What do you want me to do?"

The female voice on the phone said, "Who the hell is Joe West and what does he have to do with this?"

Mowers replied, "It's his granddaughter that your man Hector kidnapped."

The female voice said, "Aw, shit. Okay, for right now do absolutely nothing. Just keep me posted on his every move." With that the call disconnected, leaving him standing in the yard with an attitude getting worse by the minute.

Chapter Seven

Fifteen hundred miles away, General James Tracy's phone rang. His aid corporal Bruce Smith answers by saying, "General Tracy's office."

The female voice on the phone said, "I need to talk to Jim. Is he available?"

Corporal Smith replied, "Yes he is. Can I ask who's calling?"

The caller rudely replied, "No! Just get him on the phone."

Pressing the hold button, he swore, "What a bitch." He transfers the call to the general. "There's a female caller for you sir. She won't give me her name. She's on line three."

General James Tracy looked at his phone and realized it was the line reserved for the internal federal government. Picking up the phone and pressing the button, he said, "General James Tracy."

The female voice said, "Who the hell is Joe West? Why haven't I been notified about him? I need to know who he is and what he's doing and I needed to know it yesterday."

With a couple of quick keystrokes, the General replied, "I don't know. It looks like his file is sealed. Judge dead. No admittance."

The female voice replied, "Will get it open and get me the information in it. And do it now!" Without so much as a goodbye the line went dead.

General Tracy looked at the screen in front of him and thought, "There's a leak and I need to find it. The General of the joint chiefs is going to go nuts if this gets out."

Twenty minutes later General Tracy stood at attention as he waited for General Jacobson to finish his call and acknowledge him. As he heard the General say, "Yes, Joe, that is correct." Looking up, he continued, "Okay, Commander, I'll see you then." Disconnecting the call, he looked at General Tracy and said, "Have a seat, Jim. What's on your mind?"

Looking around, he said, "I think we might have a problem coming up. I just got a call from the hill and she asked about someone she shouldn't have. Someone who's file is sealed and it says absolutely no admittance."

General Jacobson replied, "Who is she? Who is she asking about? What does she want to know?"

Jim answered, "I would rather not say who just now. Although she wants to know everything about a man named Joe West, I can tell you that much. That particular file says the judge that put it together is dead."

General Jacobson swore out loud as he said, "Just forget you ever heard that name. When she calls you back, simply tell her. You cannot get in file per my orders. She might call me. If she does, I'll take care of it."

Arriving back at his office, General Tracy picked up his phone and placed a call. A female voice answered saying, "What did you find out? I need to know everything. Can you email the file to me?"

General Tracy smiled as he thought, *She's about to go batshit crazy. Plus Jacobson is going to hate me.*

He said, "Sorry, no can do. I don't have enough clearance to get into that file. I asked General Jacobson about it and he simply said for me to forget that name."

The lady on the other end of the line started screaming, "Just who in the hell does he think he is? I'm a US Congresswoman, I have the right to know. I'll ask the president if I need to. You had better tell Jacobson that he needs to call me and call me right now."

General Tracy replied, "I'm a one star General, he's got five. I don't tell him anything. You can try, although I'm quite sure you won't like his answer." With that, Tracy disconnected the call and sat back, hooking his fingers together and starting to count. By the time he reached seven, the phone rang. Picking up the handset, he said, "General Tracy."

The lady yelled, "Go around him or over him, talk to anyone you can think of. Just get me everything you can find. Do it as soon as possible."

Disconnecting the call, General Tracy said, "Yeah, like that's going to happen. Even that nosy old bitch doesn't need to know everything."

Smiling, he shut everything down and headed towards the afternoon meeting, hoping someone else would bring up the name and he could just listen. Now his curiosity was about to get the better of him.

Arriving at the meeting of the joint Chiefs, he took his seat and waited. Listening to conversations around him, he heard the name pop up several times. *Yes,* he thought, *That old bat has gotten everyone wound up. Something tells me there's one hell of a shit storm brewing on the horizon.*

As the meeting opened, General Todd Browning said, "I got a call from Capitol hill asking about a man by the name of…" looking at his notes, he continued, "Joe West. Can anyone shed some light on this? Like, maybe about who he is?"

"The file I found says it's sealed. No admittance."

General Jacobson clears his throat as he said, "That file is sealed per my instructions and orders. It is to remain sealed. Now listen closely. I don't want anyone trying to get into it." He looked around the room, making absolutely sure he made eye contact with everyone. "Have I made myself clear?" Picking up his phone, he said, "General Jacobson here. Find the Joe West file and lock it down. Make sure absolutely no one, and I mean no one, can get into it." Listening for a minute, he continued, "Seal it per my instructions." Listening again he asked, "Who's trying to get into it?" Listen again, he said, "What do you mean you don't know? Put a trace on it. I want the name and title information of anyone and everyone that tries to get past me and into that file. Do you hear me? Now trace it." Listening again, he said, "Capital hill? Whose computer or office?" Pausing again, he continued, "Yes, I got it. Send that old bitch a message saying military eyes only. This file is totally and completely off limits to everyone. Do not try to access this file again. Repeat, do not try again. By the order of the military joint chiefs and sign it per my name." Listening again, he continued,"Yes. My name and do it now." Looking around at everyone in the room, he said, "That file is off limits to everyone. Do you all understand? Now I have work to do. Is there anything else we need to cover?" General Jacobson looked at everyone and said, "Okay, then. I'll talk to you all next week. I'm going to be out of town in the next couple of days."

Everyone in the room wanted to know where he was going and why. Although no one was about to ask. Five stars and he was mad. That made for a very bad combination in the military. His five stars put him at the very top of the food chain. Even the president didn't want to cross him and get on his bad side.

Arriving back in his office, he said, "I'm going to be busy for the next hour or so. No interruptions and I mean not one!"

Walking into his office, he closed the door. Sitting down, he looked up a number and placed a call. Fifteen hundred miles away, Joe's phone rang as he got up and walked away saying, "Yes, General?"

Listening for a few minutes, he finally said, "Yes, sir. I think a halo jump would be perfect. At forty thousand we should be above any chance of a radar intercept. Plus by the time they do pick it up, I'll be out and on my way."

General Jacobson replied, "I'll get this set up and get back to you. Now listen, half of Washington is trying to figure out just who the hell you are. I have your file sealed and locked down. It'll work for a while although sooner or later someone is going to figure it out. So get going as fast as you can. While you are in Columbia, try to get all the information we talked about. I'll need it as soon as possible. This will help insure your chances of success. I wouldn't do this for just anyone. Although that call sign ghost still carries a lot of weight and most of us older officers still remember what the world was never told. Now use that name to get onto the base when I get this all set up. Plus use it anytime you need to while on military bases. Or on this operation. This operation and your mission is absolutely top priority."

Looking around, Joe continued to walk as he said, "Mission order. First, find and save Janessa. I'll call for an extraction point. Second, get into the cartel's office. Find all the information I can on who's backing them. Then, find Kay hopefully still alive and bring her home also."

Joe looked back over his shoulder. He could see his wife sitting on the deck talking with Desiree. As the tears started trickling down his cheeks, he said, "Thank you, sir. I won't disappoint you."

General Jacobson replied, "Good luck and by the grace of God you'll survive. Once I receive word I'll set up the extraction points. The second one hopefully for two."

Joe took a deep breath and wiped the tears from his eyes. He said, "With all due respect, Sir. If I don't find Kay, I won't be coming back. Although I'll get the information to you somehow. What you do with it at that point is your decision."

General Jacobson looked at the ceiling as he said, "I've known you for over twenty years. She must be one hell of a lady to have you tied up this tight."

Turning around, he continued to watch her as he replied, "Yes, Sir. She is all of that and more. I can't imagine my life without her, Sir. I'm sure by now if it wasn't for her I would be dead."

General Jacobson said, "She sounds like one hell of a lady. I would love to meet her someday." Pausing, he continued, "I'll be sending you an email in the next couple of hours. It'll have all the information you'll need. Use your call sign as soon as you make contact with the people's names I give you. And Joe?"

"Yes, sir?"

General Jacobson said, "Be careful, son. I know you'll stick your neck out. Just make sure you can get it pulled back before the ax falls. Good luck and good hunting."

Joe replied, "Yes, Sir and thank you Sir. I promise I'll get you the information you need. The information our country needs." With that, Joe disconnected the call and stood watching Kay.

My god, he thought, *I have to figure out a way to achieve all I have to. Plus I have to bring her home. I just have to.*

Walking back, he poured a cup of coffee and sat down. He smiled at Kay while his mind raced off to a county he prayed he would never see again. Kay reached over to give him a kiss. She looked into his eyes and said, "It'll be okay. Get Janessa and then hopefully you can find me. Although please, hon. Please always remember that I love you Joe. I love more than I ever thought I could ever love a man."

Joe smiled again as he watched the tears flowing from her eyes and said, "I'll find you and bring you home." Putting his arms around her, he sat rocking back and forth. As his hand slowly stroked her hair. His mind was already days ahead and miles away as he thought about what he was about to do. What he has to do. What he has to accomplish.

A few minutes later, Agent Mowers walked out and said, "I've been told to arrest you."

Joe replied, "Arrest me? For what? I haven't done anything."

Mowers replied, "For interfering in a federal investigation."

Standing up, Joe said, "You can try, but you had better call for backup first. The last time you tried that I went easy on you. This time I won't."

Mowers stood there. Not sure if he should actually try or if he should call for backup. Or simply do as the people he had called told him to do. Stand back and keep his mouth shut. That the man he was looking at was a professional trained killer. After trying to stare Joe down, Mowers said, "Just stay out of my way and out of this investigation. Plus when Hector calls, I'll do all the talking."

Joe watched as he walked away. Looking at Kay, he said, "He can do all the talking. I've sync our two phones together. I'll hear every word. As soon as I get a location of where you are to meet I'm gone. I'll be in position at the exchange point in less than twenty four hours. I'll get set up and get Janessa as soon as I can. Then I'll watch for you. As soon as I see you I'll start a battle like they have never seen. When the first shot is fired you hit the dirt and stay down until I get to you and I will get to you. I'll get you to safety then I'm going after them. Don't worry, I lived in Columbia for nearly ten years. While it may have changed some. I'm quite sure I'll be able to find my way around."

Getting up together, they walked inside. Joe filled two coffee cups. Handing one to Kay, then turning, they both walked so they could talk with Colton and Desiree for a few minutes and walk back outside. Just as they sat down, Kay's phone rang. Looking at Mowers, Joe signaled him that the call had come in. Kay answered on the third ring saying, "Where's my granddaughter? Hector handed the phone to Janessa just long enough for her to say, "Grandma, Grandma, are you there?" Before Kay could reply, Hector said "I'll meet you in Tunja Colombia on Wednesday." The line went dead.

Joe quickly looked up the town. He remembered it as soon as the map opened. It was about in the center of the country. Thinking to himself, *It's only a few miles to Bogota. I hope the DEA has a safe house there. Hopefully he can drop Janessa with them and then locate Kay.*

Like someone had flipped a switch, Joe's mind went to hunter sniper mode, raining hell and destruction on Hector and anyone else that tried to stand between him and finding Kay. Grabbing his cell, he got up and placed the first of two calls.

Steve answered on the second ring and said, "Please, don't tell me you have caused more trouble."

Joe replied, "Nope, not yet. Hey, listen up. We just got the call from our friends in Columbia. Every time he uses his phone try to figure out where he is."

Steve replied, "I'm way ahead of you. The call he just made came from Medellin."

Still looking at the map, Joe asked, "Do you have a team anywhere close to that area? Hector wants Kay to meet him in Tunja. That has to be fifty or more miles apart. If you can, have a team hit the transfer. That should cause a riff in the cartels. They'll think it is me. With some luck they'll send every man they have to track me down. As soon as you have Janessa, haul ass to the American Embassy in Bogota. Turn Janessa over to them and have your guys melt into the city. Now remember, the cartels are going to be looking for me. A white man in a city full of dark skinned people. While the cartels are looking for me I'll hit their headquarters, the Norte del Valle Cartel. I'm quite sure all the information I'm looking for is there. As soon as I get the information I'm looking for I can send it stateside and start looking for Kay."

Steve replied, "Yes, I have a team plus a safe house if needed. My team is all Columbians and I trust each and every one of them. They'll have no problem blending in and can absolutely disappear. I'll get this all arranged and get back to you with all the information on the operation." Pausing for a couple of seconds, he added, "Operation White Dove."

Laughing, Joe replied, "Operation White Dove is about to commence. Hopefully you'll get Janessa safely to the embassy while I get the information about who's backing and helping these low lifes get their drugs into the United States. Then find Kay still alive and get both of us out."

Steve replied, "I'll get back to you via secure email as soon as I have it set up. Once Janessa is at the embassy we can start the operation." Pausing again, he continued, "Securing Bella. I think I can put together another team to help you get out of Columbia. Just keep checking your email."

Joe smiled as he replied, "Thanks, Steve. Although I won't be coming out if I don't find her."

Disconnecting the call, he let his mind drift back to Colombia again. His mind went to hell on earth as he then called General Jacobson. Giving him a quick summary of his initial plan to get Janessa to the US Embassy in Bogota, then going after Kay.

General Jacobson replied, "I'll have a US Embassy bird on standby. They can safely fly her to a military transport jet. That can get her back here."

Joe stood there thinking about what he was about to do as he checked his email. Reading the one from Steve first, he smiled and thought, *Okay, operation White Dove is set. God, I pray that it works.* He opened the second email and read it. Then reads it again thinking, *Halo jump it is. Hopefully they can get me within twenty miles or so. It'll be a hike if it's farther away than that.* Looking at the number again he quickly called it.

The call was answered as the voice simply said, "Yes".

Joe took a deep breath before saying, "Code word ghost. I'll be there in a couple of hours." Pressing end, he turned and slowly walked back towards Kay, all the time watching the surroundings and thinking about the upcoming mission.

Back in Washington, an email arrived at the wrong computer. General Jeff Jacobs opened the email and started to smile as he read it, thinking no paper trail. He picked up his phone and called. "Set him up with jump gear for 35000 feet," he said to the other end, "Although the pilot climbed to 55000 to avoid radar. Have him jump a Razor. This will shorten his jump time plus we can hopefully drop him over Venezuela."

Major Bruce Evans replied, "He might not have enough supplemental oxygen."

General Jacobs said, "I've jumped a Razor many times. He'll be just fine. Oh, and have him jump AZ- 1000q92."

Major Evans replied, "Yes, sir. I'll make sure of everything. Plus, send me an email on that."

General Jacobs replied, "Yes, I'll send it when I have time. For now it's a verbal order. Just get everything set up!"

Major Evans said, "Yes, sir. I'll see to it myself." Then he thought, *Why jump that old worn out piece of shit. When we have so many new and better ones? Oh will it's not my place to ask a General to explain himself. I just follow orders."*

Disconnecting the call, Jacobs called one more number. A sarcastic woman answered and said, "You had better have good news."

Jacobs replied, "All set and as good as done. He won't survive." The lady didn't say a word. She simply disconnected the call. Smiling, Jacobs thought, *She's going to help me get my fourth star. When Jacobson retires I'll be ranking General and walk right in. General of the joint chiefs.*

Standing there, Joe looked into the beautiful eyes of the woman he loved more than life and said, "There's been several changes. I got help from the military and DEA. I'm not sure you'll actually see Janessa. So just remember this: you have to fight with everything you have. Do what they say. Just make sure you fight everything they try. Just survive, I'll find you. That I promise."

Kay stepped forward as the tears started and she broke into sobs. She said, "I know you'll try. I also know you'll die trying. If it comes to that, protect yourself first. Just always remember that I love you Joe. I'll always love you."

Joe stood there rocking from side to side although his mind was already 3000 miles away thinking about the days ahead. Could the DEA free Janessa before Hector gets Kay? He'd know when Janessa was safe. Could he then find Kay? He was sure Hector would keep Kay with him, so every time he used his phone the computer geek could trace it. He should be able to see Kay's location with their phones being synced as long as Kay had her phone. Thinking for a few minutes, he placed yet another call.

Steve answered saying, "I think I have everything in place. As soon as I get the last confirmation, I'll email you."

Joe replied, "That's fantastic. Hey, I need a micro dot satellite transmitter. Make it look like a ring. Size six and send it to the same address you sent my phone, only to Kay West. I'm leaving soon. Hopefully she'll get it tomorrow. Email me the frequency so I can sync it to this phone. Between you guys tracking her's and Hector's phones and me tracking the micro dot, hopefully I'll find her before anything really bad can happen."

Listening, Steve said, "Got it, micro dot ring size six. I'll have the geek squad get it done right away and send it out to a military carrier. I'll make sure they hand deliver it tomorrow. Directly to her and no one else."

Disconnecting the call, he started to think, *Can I get both of us out of Columbia? Can I get the information that General Jacobson wants- needs? I've put Janessa's safety in the possession of the only group of people I trust. I know they can get her to safety. Next I have to get that information for General Jacobson, then find Kay. He already knows in his mind he's going to find Kay then get the information from the cartels. Although if he's going to fail someone, something, it'll be the information part. He can't- he won't fail Kay.*

Stepping back at arms length he said, "It's showtime. You'll be flying out tomorrow. I'm flying out today. I'll be in Columbia tonight after dark. I'm jumping in as close as I can get to Tunja."

Kissing her, he walked into the house. Grabbing the duffle bag he had packed earlier, he walked back to Kay and wrapped his arms around her. He kissed her long and deep. Holding on to the very last second, he kissed her on the forehead before walking to the waiting car to take him to the airport.

Arriving at the airport, he did a walk around inspection before starting both engines and taxis to the active runway. Contacting Cherokee traffic, he pushed the throttles full forward. As the Cessna lifted off, Joe lifted the flaps and landing gears before banking slightly northwest, heading for Omaha and Offutt Air Force Base. Twenty miles out he contacted air traffic control and was given priority permission to land. In other words, to get on the ground now- they were waiting for him.

As Joe taxied up to the terminal, he was met by two airmen. They gave him all the information he needed to get to where he was headed. The one said, "We'll take care of your plane commander. It'll be in that hanger over there."

Joe glanced over his shoulder and thanked the men as he grabbed his duffle and jogged into the terminal. Meeting Lieutenant Colonel William Todd, he slid to a stop and saluted. Colonel Todd returned the salute before stepping forward and saying, "Damn, it's good to see you again. After you left Afghanistan I tried to keep up. But one day your trail just ended. I knew you were still alive but I couldn't find out where you were. After this is over maybe we can have a beer and catch up."

Joe replied, "That would be great. I would like to catch up on everything."

Colonel Todd said, "Now listen up. We have a special designed Lear waiting on you. Everything on the General's list is already inside and packed. I was told to add a few things that might come in handy. Have you ever jumped using a razor?"

Joe looked at him with a puzzled look and said, "No, sir. I have jumped many times although I have no idea what a razor is."

Stopping Colonel Todd says," You're a pilot, right?"

Joe replies, "Yes, sir."

Colonel Todd said, "Strap it on and jump. You'll absolutely love it. It's all computer controlled with altitude and speed sensors so it'll deploy automatically. Then you simply fly it on a compass heading to your destination. Only one thing, before you let go of it and start your free fall, make sure to point it at the ocean. It's designed to be recovered and used again and again. Now in a free fall you drop at about one hundred miles per hour. This sweet little beauty slips through the air at close to two hundred miles per hour while dropping only five hundred feet per hour. It's a single man high speed glider. We are going to drop you just outside the Columbian air space at thirty five thousand feet. We shouldn't be on their radar or their airspace for more than a few minutes if at all. The razor has a radar cross section of a hummingbird so they won't see you coming. I've talked with General Jacobson several times. This is a fantastic thing you are doing and I know your country will thank you." Stepping back, he then saluted Joe and continued, "Good luck and good hunting. Oh, and Randy? Please be careful son."

Joe returned the salute. Turning, he looked at the blacked out Lear and thought, "Oh my god. Black ops again. I'm going back to hell."

Climbing aboard, he sat down, strapped in, and put on the headset. A voice came over the headset saying, "Welcome aboard, Ghost. This is Captain Casper. We should be over your drop point in seven hours. Get some sleep. I'll wake you an hour out so you have time to get set up."

Joe chuckled as he thought, *I'm going back to hell and I have a comedian taking me.*

As the Lear lifted off, Joe got up and started going through the equipment, checking and rechecking everything. He strapped on his two pistols and knives, double checking his sniper rifle and M-16 plus ammunition. With everything ready, he sat down, relaxed and slowly fell asleep.
He slipped through the jungle. It was a completely black night, heavy overcast with no moon. Randy knew the trail and he had walked it several times. It led to Medellin and it also led to Gabriella. He's walked this trail so many times that he made turns without realizing it.

As he arrived in Medellin, he sat and watched. There was no one out. It was nearly two in the morning. Slowly, he made his way through town to his destination. Waiting in the shadows, he watched. No one was moving.

He had told Gabriella he would be back tonight. They had made plans and would slip off together for a few days before he would have to leave again. Something didn't feel right. The front door looked to be open. He didn't understand, her papa was much more careful than that.

Lifting his M-16, he slowly approached the door. It had been busted open with one of the hinges broken. Looking inside, he nearly puked. It was a bloodbath.

Gabriella, her mama, and her papa were laying in a bloody pile on the floor. Going up the steps two at a time, he kicked her bedroom door open to find her naked body laying on the bed with the words puta puta carved across her chest. Randy slowly walked up to the bed and lifted her in his arms, blankets and all and carried her body downstairs, placing her on the floor next to her parents. Carefully, he arranged them all next to each other and then covered their bodies. Taking two white phosphorus grenades, he opened the basement door and pulled the pins as he tossed them. Closing the basement door, he walked over and kneeled next to Gabriella, kissing her forehead as he said a prayer and covered her up.

Turning to look at the basement door as it was blown across the kitchen, he stood up and walked out. He was done hiding, now walking down the middle of the street. He wanted a fight. He could see the light as the fire grew, casting more and more light in the pitch black night. Just a few feet from the jungle he turned back to look. The house was totally engulfed in flames. There would be no evidence left. She wasn't a whore as the cartels had said. Standing there he thought, *Punta, my ass. Not by a damn sight.*

It wasn't the end, it was the beginning. They had just made it personal and they would pay for this. They would pay dearly. She wasn't a whore and he had loved her, although that was something he would never admit.

Joe woke to the sound of someone saying, "Ghost, Ghost, your drop point is an hour and fifteen minutes out. I have coffee up here if you want some."

Joe smiled as he thought, "Wow, a comedian with brains. Coffee." As he entered the cockpit, he looked at the pilot and said, "Captain Casper, I presume?"

The captain smiled as he offered his hand and said, "Actually, it's Captain Alex Esperanza. My Copilot tonight and most nights is Jane Rodriguez."

Shaking both of their hands, Jane handed him a cup and said, "That door drops into a seat. Sit down while we go over a few things. Have you ever jumped a razor? It's a fun little sled, just be careful not to exceed 300, it has a tendency to rip off a wing or two. Don't spin it, it'll flatten out and you cannot recover. Don't let it stall, it drops the right side real severely and you'll end up inverted hard to get back on top when you're dangling from it. Before you kick free, point it at the ocean. When your weight leaves there's a small flight computer. It will take over everything and it should make it back. It has a homing beacon so that way it can be recovered. We don't know anything about your mission, so all we can say is good luck Commander."

Chapter Eight

Joe stopped and looked back. "You two have a safe flight home."

Jane replied, "We are not going home. At least, not right away. There's some scuttling but going around that we may be picking up a VIP. We've been given clearance to head for Venezuela for a few days."

Joe smiled as he thought about the email he had received about an embassy bird flying Janessa to a military jet. Looking from Alex to Jane, he said, "Enjoy your off time." Turning, he then headed back to finish suiting up and setting up for the jump, checking and rechecking his equipment. When he was ready, he looked at his wrist altimeter.

He was set to jump at thirty five thousand feet. Although the wrist altimeter says 55,000. Thinking quickly, he realized it was about 70 below zero outside right now. As he headed for the cabin, the green jump light came on and the door opened. Joe disconnected from the plane's oxygen and checked his. With one deep breath, he was out the door and dropping at nearly one hundred miles and hour.

In the matter of a few seconds, he realized something was not right. The razor was supposed to self deploy. Looking for a manual override, he felt a need for more oxygen. *What the hell is wrong?* he thought, as he dropped earth ward. Not finding an over ride or anything else that might help fix the problem, he tried to unbuckle the safety harness, pushing the release several times with nothing happening. He was strapped to a two hundred pound carbon fiber missile.

The razor wouldn't drop nose down and it was slowing its descent. He could see his vision as it moved in and the fear of losing consciousness came forward. Knowing he had only a few minutes before his world went black, he found his knife. With two quick movements, he cut through the safety harness and kicked the razor away. Joe struggled to get the knife put away as he thought of Kay. He had failed her. His world went black.

Joe's eyes slowly started to open. Reaching, he pushed the purge button on the regulator. A surge of oxygen hit his system as ever so slowly his senses start coming back. Looking around, he could see stars then nothing but blackness. Again, he saw stars then blackness. *I'm tumbling,* he thought as he pressed the purge valve again. Trying to get into a free fall position to stabilize his descent was his first thought. With his arms out, he couldn't straighten out his legs. Doubling back up and starting to tumble again, he ran his hands down one leg then the other, finding that the safety harness that had held him in the razor was now wrapped around his leg. Reaching for his knife he quickly cuts through the harness. Moving the knife to his right hand, he got the blade closed as his left hand found the release for his parachute. Looking at his wrist altimeter again, he tried to calculate how long he had been dropping. Seeing a light in the distance, he pulled the chute.

The fantastic snap came to his ears. It was the sound of a fully deployed chute opening above him. For the first time since jumping, he took a deep relaxing breath.

Looking down into the blackness of the Columbian jungle, he knew he was off course although there was nothing he could do about that at the moment. Pulling his pack up, he positioned it between his legs. Then crossing his legs, he prepared to land. The pack should have helped stop anything sharp from going any farther up, which of course includes him. Then he flipped his night vision goggles into place- nothing but jungle. Not a light for miles in any direction. Removing the goggles, he felt the first of several branches as he dropped through the jungle canopy. Hanging by the chute lines, he started to swing, getting closer and closer to the nearest tree. Finally, his right hand found a branch on the next swing as he got a better grip and hung on. Slowly, he pulled himself up and in. Getting a firm grip on the tree, he tripped the release and let the parachute harness fall away.

Finding a few large strong branches, he positioned himself to get as comfortable as possible. Then looping a strap around the tree, he laid back and caught a few hours of sleep. Joe's internal alarm went off just a few minutes before five am. He sat up thinking about what he had to do. Reaching into his pack, he found the small thermos of coffee Jane had handed him just as he was saying goodbye. Pouring some into the thermos cap, he watched as the shadows changed on the jungle floor. He watched a Jaguar slip through an opening and disappear into the shadows. A sloth slowly moved above him and off to his right. As daylight invaded the jungle, he worked his way to the ground. Opening his phone, he hit the power switch and waited. Checking his email, he sent a message to both Steve and General Jacobson saying he was on the ground and headed toward Norte del Valle Cartel in Buenaventura.

Looking at the map, he figured with luck he would be in position the following day at about noon. Picking up his phone, he checked the email and sent one more to Steve asking if everything was set and ready to get Janessa. Joe could be in position at about noon. If this works he should be able to walk in without too much trouble and have plenty of time to find the information. Pressing send, he powered off the phone to save the battery. Grabbing his equipment, he headed for Buenaventura while his thoughts and prayers were with Kay.

Just before noon the following day, he stopped on a sunny hillside overlooking Buenaventura. Powering up the phone, he saw an email from Steve. Opening it, he quickly read that Operation White Dove was set for today. They had already located the car and were tracking it. Although Hector called Kay's phone and from what they could tell he was not with Janessa, he was already in Tunja. Kay wouldn't be there for another couple of hours. They asked when they should hit transer.

Kay's plane had landed in Bogota. Just as she cleared customs she was met by two of Hector's men. The two men grabbed her arms and half-carried half-dragged her out the terminal and to a waiting van. As the side door opened, they roughly threw her through the door. In a few minutes, Kay was on her way to meet Hector and was in more danger than she ever thought possible.

Joe read the message several times. Looking at his phone, he located Kay. Her ring was showing her location within a few feet. She had already left Bogota. She would be in Tunja in an hour or so.

Thinking quickly, he typed back: **Yes, absolutely. Hit it and get her to the embassy as fast as possible. I'm sure Hector will keep Kay with him. As long as Janessa is safe, Operation White Dove is a success and I can get started on the rest of this nightmare. I'm in position and can see Norte del Valle Cartel in Buenaventura. When you hit the transfer all hell should break loose. I'm sure that Pablo will send everyone he can to Bogota trying to find me. Bogota is a large city. He'll hold them there looking for me as long as the cartel will allow.**

Pressing send, Joe found the small solar charger plugging in the phone. He sat back and tried to relax as he waited for the news on Operation White Dove.

Sixty-three miles away an old man leading a horse drawn wagon started across the road directly in front of a late model BMW sedan. The BMW slowed to let the man and wagon cross the road.

 Four men came out of the woods, a Chevrolet Impala slid to a stop directly behind. The man in the back seat of the BMW jumped out and opened up with a submachine gun, hitting two of the guys on foot just as the driver of the Chevrolet killed the man by the car with two well placed shots, one to his chest the second hitting him in the throat.

The man grabbed his throat and with blood spurting through his fingers, he dropped to his knees before pitching forward face first onto the road. The driver of the BMW and the other guy in the front seat instantly grabbed for their guns as one of the men on foot shot and killed the driver. The young lady in the back seat threw her arms around the passenger and using the plastic cuffs binding her wrist she placed her feet against the back seat and pulled with everything she had, all the while cursing a blue streak.

The passenger of the Chevrolet was out and moving just as the car slid to a stop. With his knife, he cut the plastic cuffs and the guy's throat with one quick slash while the driver hurried to help the two injured to the car.

The man leading the horse watched. He smiled as he slowly led the horse away down the gravel road. The Impala sped away from the scene and headed towards Bogota and the US embassy. In less than sixty seconds, part one of Operation White Dove was over.

Joe's phone beeped, notifying him of an incoming email. Picking up his phone, he read: **Operation White Dove is a success. She's on her way. We are tracking Kay and should arrive in Tunja within the hour.** About twenty minutes later, a second email came in. Joe quickly opened and started to swear as he read: **I was just notified that White Dove's car was hit. White Dove missing. No survivors. Repeat, no survivors. White Dove not among the casualties. We failed. I have men on the ground in the area. What do you want me to do?**

Thinking for a minute, he said out loud, "We have a spy. Someone has notified the cartels. I wonder how much they know?"

Slowly and carefully, he wrote a reply, **Gather intel. See if they can find out where she is being held. I'm heading for Bogota as fast as I can. As soon as you find out, let me know.**

Joe read the message twice. Pressing send, he picked up his binoculars and watched. Less than an hour later the cartel's home office exploded with activity. Smiling, he thought *maybe, just maybe.*

Joe watched from a grassy hillside as car after car left the villa and headed in a southwestern direction. Quickly, he packed up his equipment thinking, *They are sure I'm in Bogota. This should give me several hours to get in and find what I'm looking for and get out.*

Joe sat and waited on the hillside, preparing and waiting for darkness. He could see only a few guards and they seemed to be lazy or maybe just complaisant thinking he was in Bogota and probably running for his life. These guys looked too young to remember the ghost of Columbia. As he sat there, he saw his opening. Twenty minutes later, Joe carefully walked across the lawn towards the one guard that was still outside singing in Spanish.

Only ten feet away, a flick of his left hand and a knife appeared in the man's throat. As he dropped to the ground, Joe grabbed the grip and a slight twist as he pulled it from the man's throat. There was a spray of blood followed by a gurgling sound. Wiping the blade on a nearby curtain, he headed inside in search of the other four.

Twenty minutes later, the last man died as Joe's suppressed glock popped twice. The guard fell backwards into the pool. Joe slowly looked around as he walked the pool side and watched as the man sank, blood trailing from the two holes in his chest.

Walking through the house, he started searching for the office. Finding a locked door, he stopped, stepping back and kicking it open. Seeing a desk and cabinets, the search started. Thirty minutes later, the cabinets were empty and he found nothing.

Next, he started searching the desk. Finding a locked drawer, one bullet opened it. There was a checkbook and a register. Opening the register, he started to read. "Yes," he uttered, "Names I recognize." Taking the register, he kept looking. Finding a key ring with only one strange looking key, he picked it up.

Walking around the room, he looked behind all of the pictures. In the bathroom, he opened the closet and pulled everything out and onto the floor. Back out in the office, he tipped over both cabinets.

Under one he saw a door. Opening the door and slipping the key in the slot, he carefully opened the floor safe. Taking several thousand dollars in cash, both US dollars and Mexican Pesos, he put it in his backpack.

Picking up a bank bag, he removed the contents. As he started to read, a smile came to his face. Names, dates, more names, more dates. Anglo Saxton names, American names. More names he recognized along with bank information, transfer dates, and amounts.

Joe smiled as he put the information in his backpack and walked out thinking, *This should be enough to cause one hell of a shit show in Washington.*

Slipping out the door, Joe stayed in the shadows. Looking around, he saw a couple of Range Rovers. Opening the door, he found the keys in the first one. Ten minutes later he was several miles down the road. Backing into a side road, he got as far as possible while still being able to see the road and killed the engine. Sitting in the dark, he thought for a minute. *I have to figure out who's getting the information to the cartels.*

Slowly, he composed an email to the general: **I'm doing one thing at a time. The information you need is the closest. I'll watch the house and get it first. That'll give Steve and his team time to try and find White Dove. Fat ass Pablo knows I'm in the area. He's greedy and wants the ransom the cartels are offering for me. That should give me a slight advantage. While they are out looking for me I'll get the information. Get it sent to you. Then find White Dove. After that I'll spend whatever time I need to find Kay and bring her home. Or I'll die here in Colombia.**

Four thousand miles away, General Jacobs read an email sent to him by General Jacobson aid. Smiling, he forwarded it to an FBI agent and to an office in the House of Representatives on Capitol Hill.

About two hours later, several cars went past and headed for the compound. Waiting a few more minutes, he sent Steve an email saying: **We have a leak. Find it and patch it. It's in the pentagon and has something to do with General Jacobson. From now on I trust you and only you. I'll include you in the group emails. You'll also get the truth in a single. If you are double crossing me I'll hunt you down. You cannot run far enough or hide well enough to stop me.**

Pressing send, Joe waited a few minutes for a reply. If Steve was the leak, then he wouldn't reply, nor would he ever reply again.

Less than two minutes later, Steve's reply came back: **I'm not the leak although I'll do my best to find it. I have the perfect .40 caliber patch.**

Joe smiled as he headed for Bogota and Janessa.

An hour later, Joe received an email from Steve. Joe read out loud, "White Dove located. Location to follow. Five known armed guards. Hector, Juan, or Pablo not seen. Kay is in Tunja. Phone still activated. No calls from Hector. Have a lead on a leak. Will advise later. Good hunting Commander." Joe quickly typed the location into his GPS. Then checking the magazines in both pistols, he turned left and headed towards his granddaughter.

Sitting across the street from where Janessas was being held, he watched and waited. He knew he couldn't simply go busting in. He needed to be absolutely quiet and deadly. Three AM was the witching hour and he knew that. People could stay awake, although everyone started having trouble about two and by three their sleep deprived minds started to slow down. Judgment slowly left and was replaced by periods of being in a daze. Not sleeping although also not fully awake. Looking around, he rescinded the seat and drifted off. His dreams went immediately to Kay. The first time he saw her, the red and black outfits she was wearing. Although her eyes kept dancing in front of him. The softness of her skin when they shook hands. The look in her eyes when he lifted her chin and kissed her. Oh her lips, her fantastic lips, and the feeling of her tongue in his mouth.

My god, he thought, as his eyes opened. Looking at his watch, it was ten minutes after two. It would take him a few minutes to get inside. Once more, he checked the magazines in both pistols, then the four razor-sharp throwing knives.

 Picking up his phone, he sent Steve another email: **I need the personal emails of the two drivers that brought me down here. Send them as soon as you can. With a little luck I'll have White Dove in about twenty minutes. I really need them to meet me.**

Pressing send, he carefully opened the door and walked across the street and up to the front door. They would expect him to come in the back or maybe from the roof. Who in their right mind would make a single person frontal attack on at least five armed guards? The first guard never felt a thing. Nor would he ever. He was sleeping in a chair just out of sight of the front door.

The suppressed 9MM in Joe's hand popped and the 147 grain hit the man just left of the center of his forehead. He never woke up. He was slammed backwards then simply slumped over and slid to the ground.

Shaking his head, Joe thought, *One down, three, probably, four to go.*

Removing his boots, he slipped stocking footed up the stairs, staying as close to the edge as possible. Not making a sound, he slowly opened the second floor door.

Listening, he heard something like someone begging and crying. As quickly yet quietly as possible, he started down the hall, stopping at each door he came to. At the fifth door he saw a man tearing a girl's pants off. With the young lady laying on her back with her legs already open, he started trying to push himself inside. He never finished that attempt as Joe all in one fluid motion grabbed him by the hair, pulling up and off of his granddaughter as he drew a razor sharp knife across his throat before pushing him to the side and covering Janessa's mouth before she had a chance to register what had just happened.

With his hand still over her mouth, he continued to whisper "Janessa, Janessa. It's me, Grandpa Joe. Look, Janessa, look it's me. It's Grandpa Joe." As soon as she realizes it was Joe and not the scum bucket trying to rape her, she burst into tears and hugged Joe so tightly he couldn't breathe. Slowly, he removed his weight from her and realized she was completely naked. Looking around, he saw a blanket. Getting up, he quickly grabbed the blanket and handed it to her while looking for her clothing. Gathering her clothing, he quickly handed it to her and said, "Hurry now. There are still at least three more guards in here. I've killed two. Although I was told at least five. We have to hurry." In the matter of a few minutes, Janessa was dressed. Sitting down, she started putting her shoes on. Joe placed his hand on her and whispered, "Carry them." Pointing at his stocking covered feet. Then placing his finger across his lips he mouthed the word, "Quiet."

Grabbing her by the hand, he quickly led her to the bed that was in the corner and told her to lay down. Taking the blanket, he then covered her before slipping across the room to stand behind the open door.

Slowly, the third guard walked in. Seeing the blanket on the bed, he started to relax as he turned to see the deadman lying against the wall a few feet away. Hearing something, he spun but it was too late for him to react. Joe drove a knife up into his lower jaw, angling back, then giving the knife a twist, severing his brain stem and killing him instantly. Catching the falling body, Joe lowered him to the floor and whispered, "Janessa, come on, let's get the hell out of here."

Jumping up, Janessa ran towards Joe. Stopping, she kicked the man that tried to rape her several times. Then turning, she followed Grandpa Joe out the door. Together, they slipped down the stairs. Just as Joe reached for the door it opened. Joe's suppressed glock jumped twice as the man fell backwards and the door slowly closed.

Looking at Janessa, he said, "Plug your ears, open your mouth, and close your eyes," as he tossed a flash bang stun grenade into the room. As the flash bang went off, Joe opened the door and his glock started to jump, spraying fire and death into the remaining guards. Janessa stumbled as she looked at the dead bodies. Joe slowed just long enough to grab his boots before running across the road. Joe took a quick look around as he opened the door of the Range Rover.

Starting the engine, he quickly checked to make sure Janessa was buckled in. Then he quickly but calmly drove out of Bogota, putting as much country behind them as possible before daybreak.

Finding a place to hide until after dark, Joe said, "Try and get some sleep. It's going to be hot later. Although we should be able to get three, maybe four hours before it gets so hot we can't stand to be in here with the windows up." Reclining her seat, Janessa was asleep in a few minutes. Joe checked his email hoping for a reply from Steve. Seeing nothing, he reclined his seat and was soon out also.

As the day progressed, the temperature started to climb. Soon Joe was awake and a few minutes later Janessa woke up trying to get the door open. The heat and humidity were climbing fast as the sun and it was only mid morning. Joe started the engine, turned on the air conditioning and said, "We need to find a safer place to hide for a while."

Slowly, he drove to the highway, looking to turn east away from Bogota and the trouble he had already caused there.

Finding a small village, Joe saw a motel sign. He said in perfect Spanish, "I need a room." When the man behind the desk asked for identification, Joe grabbed the guest book and signed Juan Ortiz's. The manager looked at the name thinking it was one of Hector's men or possibly a relative; he handed Joe a key and walked away. Not wanting any trouble with Hector, Joe dropped a handful of pesos on the counter and walked out with the key.

Getting into the room, he told Janessa, "Go take a shower. It might be a couple of days before you get a chance to take another one."

Watching as she headed for the bathroom and closed the door, Joe opened his pack. Removing a collapsible stock M16, he checked the magazine and put it on the chair next to the table by the door. Then he checked the magazines in both pistols again, placing one on the night stand between the two beds and the other in his shoulder holster.

As Janessa came out of the bathroom, she looked at all the guns and asked, "Grandpa? Are we going to be alright?"

Joe put his arm around her and said, "I promised your Grandma and your Mom and Dad I would get you home safely and that, young lady, is exactly what I'm going to do."

Picking up one of the glocks, he dropped the magazine and worked the action. Looking at Janessa, he said, "Here, can you shoot this?"

Janessa took the gun, pushed the magazines in and hit the release with her thumb. Looking at Grandpa Joe, she said, "Yes, I can. I still remember from when you took us shooting." Helping her get the hip holster in place, he said, "You sit here and be very quiet. I'm going to take a quick shower then we can both try and get a little more sleep."

Five minutes later, Joe walked out of the shower to see Janessa sitting on the edge of the bed. Looking around, he asked, "Is everything okay?"

Janessa replied, "Yes. I never heard a thing. Only your phone beeped. There's an email, only it's to Randy Jackson. Grandpa, who's Randy Jackson?"

Thinking quickly, Joe replied, "That's my code name while I'm down here looking for you. That email is from a friend I used to work with."

Opening his phone, he saw an email from Steve that read: **Drivers email to follow. Tell drivers to contact Jacobson at this email address with any questions. He will give them whatever clearances they want.**

Joe quickly copied and pasted the email address for captain Esperanza then copied the body of the email and followed by saying: **Small airport at Yopal runway about 2500 feet. I know that tight for you jet jockeys can you do it? In and out?**

His reply from Captain Esperanza came almost instantly saying: **Low and slow with room to go. Coming in short field takeoff going out. Already have clearance from Jacobson. See you tomorrow, Commander.**

Looking at his granddaughter, he said, "I have a few things to do. Why don't you try and get a little more sleep?"

Crawling into bed, she watched as Joe started taking pictures and said, "Grandpa, what are you doing?"

Joe replied, "I have to take pictures of all this paperwork and email it to a few people in the states."

Janessa said, "You can scan it in about a third of the time. It'll be absolutely clear and it's also a legal document. A picture isn't."

Joe looked up and said, "Okay, so how do I scan it?"

Janessa got out of bed and said, "You lay them all flat. I'll scan them with your phone and help you set up all the emails. That way we can both get a few more hours of sleep."

Two hours later they had scanned all 367 pages and put several emails together each containing about half because of the size of each file. Although he emailed it in full to himself at home and all eight files to Logan with instructions to forward to Adrain Sawyer if he didn't come back from Columbia.

The emails were set up to go to certain areas of the government. Federal employees went to Steve and Chance. Military to Colton and General Jacobson's private email. This way he hoped he had guaranteed some safety for himself.

Two hundred miles to the northeast, a team of navy seals were tracking a recovery beacon. Climbing a near vertical rock wall, they ended their search. The razor that Commander Randy Jackson jumped was busted beyond any chance of repair and laying on a sheer rock wall some 250 feet above the crashing waves below. The team leader removed the beacon and all flight information and US markings.

Then taking several pictures, he emailed them to General Jacobs and General Jacobson along with a message saying: **Razor located. All flight data and markings removed. Razor is busted up beyond repairable. No sign of body. Razor laying on a cliff edge. Awaiting further instructions.**

General Jacobson smiled as he read. He knew Randy was very much alive and in Colombia, although that was a secret between him and Steve. Everyone else believed him to be missing and presumed dead.

Picking up his phone, he called Steve and said, "Seal had got the razor. They did precisely as I told them. If Jacobs is leaked, he'll be a Private before Randy gets back. That's if he doesn't end up in Leavenworth."

Steve shook his head as he replied, "That's perfect. Now for the rest of this nightmare, I sure hope everything else goes as planned."

General Jacobson said, "I can't believe Jacobs, an Army General, would do something like this to one of his own men."

Steve replied, "I'm just as shocked as you are, sir. Although we did intercept a couple of his emails, one to a spam account that we tracked to the FBI building. We don't know who it is yet, although I'm sure in time we will. The other went to Capitol Hill. I got a court order to intercept all her emails with orders to forward them to the Attorney General's office."

"Perfect," replied General Jacobson. Pausing, he continued, "I sure hope he gets the information and gets it to us before something happens to him."

Steve broke in and said, "I got a message from him stating he has enough information to hang half of Washington now and possibly scare the rest into being honest for several years."

General Jacobson started to laugh as he said, "Wow, an honest politician. Now that's something new."

Steve replied, "So true, sir. Something we haven't seen in over two hundred years. Maybe it'll be a new trend. If anyone can help make that happen, it would be Randy."

Joe shook Janessa awake. It was two in the morning. It was about a three hour drive and Captain Esperanza said he would be there at dawn.

Three hours later they sat in the shadows, waiting and listening for the sounds of a military lear coming in. In the pitch black night, landing lights illuminated the sky as the black jet came over the trees, dropping nearly vertical onto the runway. Joe started the engine and headed towards the waiting lear. His senses were on full alert. With just a little luck, Janessa would be homebound in a few minutes. Off to his left, he saw lights come on and head towards him. Grabbing the M16, he pushed the gas pedal to the floor as the jet made a U turn on the runway and headed for the far end and away from the approaching cars. Joe kept the pedal floored and watched as the Lear started making its turn at the end of the runway and waited. The side door opened and Captain Esperanza jumped out, dropping to his knees with a M16 leveled at the approaching vehicles.

Joe slid to a stop and told Janessa, "Get to that plane. Don't stop, don't look back. I'll be right behind you." He knew she would either stop or slow down if she knew he wasn't coming.

Joe opened fire at the two vehicles headed in his direction, shattering the windshield in the first with several three shot bursts. Just as Esperanza opened up on the second, he watched in horror as a rocket propelled grenade streaked through the predawn, narrowly missing the jet and detonating in the jungle beyond.

Janessa dove through the door, followed a few seconds later by Captain Esperanza as the jet throttles were pushed full forward. Joe kept the second car pinned down. He continued to pour cover fire into the two cars. Looking over his shoulder, he saw the jet nose lift as it gained speed and just before the end of the runway the pilot pulled it skyway in a nearby vertical takeoff.

Joe smiled. Janessa was safe and heading home. Changing magazines, he used one hand and continued to pour cover fire at the two cars as he got into the Land Rover. He hit the starter, dropping the spent magazine and pushing a loaded one in. Thumbing the release, he stuck the barrel out the window and with one hand driving, he opened up again as he raced past. With the selector still on three shot bursts, he continued to trip the trigger and emptied yet another magazine.

On the jet, Janessa screamed, "Grandpa Joe! Grandpa Joe!" and then bursted into tears as she watched the Land Rover race away.

Running to the pilot's compartment through tear filled eyes, she screamed, "Stop! Turn around! Grandpa Joe didn't get to the plane! I saw him driving away! Go back! Go back! We have to get Grandpa Joe!"

Jane looked at Esperanza and said, "I'll go talk to her." Releasing her fight harness, she slipped from her seat. Hugging Janessa, she said, "We knew he wasn't coming. He told us to get you to safety."

Janessa replied, "I don't care what he said. Turn this thing around and go back. Those people are trying to kill him!"

Jane reached out, pulled her close, and said, "I didn't know anything about your Grandpa Joe, as you call him, other than the fact he's a Commander. That means he outranks us. He told us what to do and we have absolutely no choice but to follow the orders he gives and do exactly what he says. Although I will tell you that he is now going after your Grandma."

"My Grandma?" replied Janessa. "What is my Grandma doing here?"

"She traded herself for you," Jane replied, "to make sure you were safe. Grandpa Joe set up most everything that happened. He did what had to be done to insure your safety. Now it's our job to keep you safe and get you home."

Tears continued to flow from Janessa's eyes as Jane slowly walked her backwards. Getting her into a seat, she buckled her seatbelt and kissed her forehead and then went back to the cockpit.

Slipping back into the copilot seat, she quickly scanned the instruments as she buckled herself in and said, "Where are we?"

Esperanza replied, "We just got wet feet and are over the gulf. I already sent Jacobson a message telling him that we have White Dove and are headed north. I gave him our estimated arrival time at Andrews."

Joe didn't slow down until he was miles down the road. Pulling onto a side road, he drove around a corner and out of sight. Getting out his ammunition, he started loading magazines.

With everything loaded, he sent Steve a quick email: **White Dove headed home. Part one of this nightmare is complete. I watched until the drivers were totally out of sight. Now starts part two: rescuing Bella.**

Pressing send, he reclined the seat for a few hours of sleep.

A few hours later, Joe woke to a beeping sound.

Picking up his cell, the message read: **Bella's phone went active for just a few seconds. A few minutes later, Hector placed a call from the same area. Both phones went dead although we got a location. It looks like they are in Medellin as of fifteen minutes ago.**

Joe reads the message a second time. Reaching for the key he thought, *I hope her phone goes active again. It's about a two hour drive.*

Arriving in Medellin, Joe parked on a side street where he could watch the city center.

He wrote a quick email: **Arrived in Medellin, waiting for any further information you can get. Remote access Bella's phone and try to activate it. Give me the GPS quadrants. Her ring isn't transmitting anymore.**

Steve read the email then looked at the computer analyst. He said, "He wants to try and access Kay's phone remotely. To get its location. Is that possible? How long will it take?"

Joan tapped a few keys as she said, "If the battery is in it, then say, ten seconds to power up, fifteen seconds to find itself, ten seconds to get location, and five seconds to shut down. If no one is watching it, less than a minute and it'll go black again."

Steve looked at the ceiling for a minute and said, "What if someone is watching?"

Joan replied, "He'll probably walk into a trap."

Looking at his computer, he wrote a quick email to Jacobson explaining what was about to happen and what the consequences could be.

General Jacobson's reply came back a few minutes later: **Do it, but say a prayer. I think he needs all the help he can get.**

Steve read the email twice. Pausing for a moment, he looked at the ceiling. Taking a deep breath, he looked at Joan, nodded and said, "It's a go."

With several keystrokes, Joan accessed Kay's phone. Powering it up and turning on her GPS, she gave the phone time to locate itself and send a location and then shut itself down. It all took just over a minute. Looking at Steve, she said, "I just sent you an email copied directly from Kay's phone. The location was picked up by three towers so it should be within a hundred feet and probably less. You can simply add what you want to say and forward it to Randy. Yes, I know who you are talking to. It's one of the perks of the job. Don't worry, General Jacobson knows me and that's the biggest reason I'm doing this. He trusts me completely, without question."

Steve read the location and sent the email. Ten minutes later, Joe was reading it and punching the location into his GPS. Kay was just over four miles away, clear on the other side of town. Joe knew he couldn't move until it was dark so he parked the Range Rover in a shopping mall and walked a short distance to a motel, signing the guest book as Miguel Ortiz. He paid in pesos and went to the room, settling down and trying to get a few hours of sleep, praying they wouldn't go anywhere until the following day. Hopefully by then he would have Kay and be running for the border or the coast.

Sleep didn't come easily. Dreams bombarded his mind. First Afghanistan, then the jungles of Columbia. He saw Kay in his dreams. Always just out of his reach, try as he could, he just couldn't get to her. Waking, Joe shook his head and then headed for the shower. It was just after midnight. *Time to go*, he told himself.

He took a quick shower and he was out the door. Joe looked at himself in the mirror. Dying his hair and the beard had worked. He didn't look anything like the Joe West in his passport picture. Checking the magazines for his glock, he slipped it back into his shoulder holster. Then taking the H and K from his right side holster, he checked the magazine. Working the action, he slipped it back into the holster grip forward for quick and easy cross draw. Grabbing his backpack he was out the door and moving. Looking at his GPS, it was about four miles to Kay. The two blocks to the mall parking lot took forever. He was this close yet so far away. Was she still alive and unharmed? She had to be. With everything they had been through, it couldn't end like this. He would find her and bring her home.

Arriving at the mall parking lot, he stood in the shadows and watched. Looking for movement, anything that just didn't look right. Seeing a flash of light, Joe carefully backed out and circled the lot. Coming up from behind, he could see two guys sitting in the dark and watching the Land Rover. Joe slowly scanned the area. Was there more than one team? Or maybe multiple teams working the city? A sort of mobile guard system moving through the city trying to locate him before he could get to Kay? Janessa was safe and out of the country, so Hector couldn't use that threat anymore.

Leaving his backpack, Joe removed his boots and stocking feet. He slipped up behind the two guards without making a sound. The first guard died where he sat as Joe covered his mouth and pushed the eight-inch blade at an angle up and back at the same time. With a quick twist of his wrist, severing the brain stem, the guy was dead and slipped through Joe's arms to the ground. The second guard died on his feet as Joe's left hand slashed through the air in a hooking arc. The eight-inch blade below his fist slashing the man's throat before he could sound an alarm.

Looking through their supplies, Joe grabbed their guns and ammunition. Picking up their phones, he put them on the bench and stuck his knife through them, thinking, *The number you have reached is now out of order. Please check the number and try again. If you think this is a mistake please consult the operator.*

Staying in the shadows, Joe slipped away, no alarm sounded and two more assholes died. He was sure there was another team somewhere watching the parking lot. He had finished what he wanted. The ghost was in the area. Fear the darkness, fear the night. Two-man teams will change to four. Making fewer teams also makes them easier to locate although mostly to fear the dark.

Thanks to shadows and allies, Joe made his way through the city. An hour later he was standing outside Kay's last known position. Watching the parking lot, he carefully walked through, looking for a vehicle with keys. Finding one, he looked around, keeping the location in his mind he worked his way back to the whore house Kay should be in.

Hector knew Joe was there and close. No alarm had been sounded, he just knew it and that made him nervous. Joe was hunting him.

No, he thought, *He was hunting Kay. And I'm hunting Joe.*

Just laying and waiting for Joe to make that one mistake, then he would pounce. Just like a cat waiting for that bird to get just a little closer, Hector waited. He had set up teams to watch the city. An early warning system to notify him that Joe was there and headed his way.

Smiling, Hector looked at Kay and said, "I know Joe is in the area. Soon he'll be dead and I'll have you all to myself. I won't have to continuously look over my shoulder wondering if he's there or waiting up ahead somewhere."

Kay snapped around and asked, "How do you know Joe's here?"

Hector replied, "He got your granddaughter away from me. I'm sure she would have sold for several thousands of dollars at the auction. Young and beautiful with a fantastic body. I should have had her while I had the chance. Now I'm going to kill him and get my money back from you. First personally and then I sell you."

Kay looked at Hector and said, "I'll die before you ever get to enjoy me. I'll fight until you have no choice but to kill me!"

Hector stood up and walked across the room. Without any warning, he closed his hand into a fist and punched Kay.

Kay's eyes rolled up and she dropped to the floor. Calling to one of the guards, he said, "Throw her into a room and lock the damn door. I'll deal with her later."

Joe stuck the point of his knife against the door bolt applying a little pressure. In seconds, he knew it was not a deadbolt style lock and a few moments later he was walking down the hall.

Carrying a flashlight with a red filter, flashing it into every room. The red glow didn't disrupt the sleeping people. The third door he came to was locked. Looking at the door, he realized it opened in. Smiling, he slipped a stiff plastic card and slowly opened the door. As he scanned the room, the red light stopped on the bed. There was someone lying in a strange position. A position that you normally would not sleep in. He relocked and closed the door.

Moving closer, he looked. The woman was the same size as Kay. Dark hair and the same body. Joe carefully touched the woman and slowly rolled her into a position where he could see her face. He gasped as he looked at her. Then his eyes focused and her once beautiful face came into view. She's been beaten so badly you couldn't even recognize her. Joe knew it was Kay. Several tears slipped from his eyes. As he stood there he saw something shiny on the table next to the bed. Something that was reflecting the red light. Reaching down, he picked up a diamond ring. He had never seen this ring before. Although he knew exactly what it was. He had Steve get this ring for Kay. It was the ring with the transmitter. Looking at the bed again he was now convinced the lady laying there was Kay. Lifting her left hand, he slipped the ring on the third finger of her left hand. It slid easily into place.

Looking at her again, he now knew he had failed. Failed to keep his promise to always protect her. His mind drifted to the pain of her last minutes. With his attention on Kay, he failed to hear the footsteps in the hall as a voice called out. Someone touched the door knob.

Joe stared at Kay as he heard the door open. He didn't move, his eyes were fixed on his wife. He heard the floor squeak as someone walked in. He didn't move. His eyes remained focused on Kay. Closing his eyes, he remembered her soft full beautiful lips. He heard the sound of steel sliding on leather as Hector slipped the pistol from the holster. Joe still doesn't move. With his eyes still closed, he thought about the first time he had seen her. About how he had lifted her chin to kiss her. The fantastic feeling that came over him as their tongues touched for the first time. The way that they had actually melted into each other. Neither wanting the moment to end. Thinking about all the great times they had together.

All the laughter about how she had cried the night he had asked, "Do you love me?"

Through the tears he could hear as she replied, "Yes, I think I do."

That night they had done some bar hopping and she had to pee. Stopping in the middle of nowhere. How she had yelled at Joe to help her as she tried to keep her back side out of the swamp water.

Raising his pistol, Hector smiled as he aimed and pulled the trigger. He watched as the man in front of him jerked from the impact of the bullet and fell forward.

Joe heard the popping sound as Hector's suppressed pistol went off. He heard Hector say, "Well, look at you Joe West or Randy Jackson or whatever the hell your name is. If you're the best your government has, then no wonder I've gotten away with this all these years. I won you lost, Kay is mine. All mine."

As Hector stood there soaking up the feeling of victory, he thought, *The man the cartels could not find. Could not kill. I, Hector Ortiz, found him, I trapped him. I outsmarted him.* Pausing, he thought, *I outsmarted the Ghost and I killed him. Just because he was dumb enough to love a woman. My place in the cartels will rise and someday I could be one of the leaders. I'll be a hero and always remembered as the man who killed the ghost.*

Reaching down, Hector grabbed the dead body by the hair and gave him a yank, watching as the body rolled over and fell to the floor. His mouth fell open as he realized he had killed one of his male whores.

Standing there, he heard something behind him. Slowly, he turned to stare into the ice cold blue eyes of Joe West. As his gaze slowly tried to take in everything, he saw the silenced 9 mm in Joe's left hand. Hector heard a muffled pop as a gun in Joe's hand jumped twice. He tried to lift his own gun only to have it fall from his fingers. His left hand moved to his stomach as his eyes focused on his empty right hand. *Where is my gun?* he thought. Looking at the floor he saw it. *How did it get down there?*

Slowly, he dropped to his knees. Then looking up once again, he met the dead cold blue eyes staring at him and heard Joe say, "My first bullet hit you in the bladder. Right now your urine is seeping through your intestinal tract, poisoning your system. If I'm not mistaken, the second one should have hit you in the liver. Slowly, you are going to bleed to death. Not as painful as I had hoped for, that part is yet to come. When the urine hits your liver or maybe I should say the bullet hole, the salt is going to cause pain. More pain than you've ever felt. That's when I'll be happy. Plus the fact you'll still live long enough to realize you are going to die. You'll have time to think about all the pain you've caused other people. Even if someone would get you to the hospital in the next hour your chances are very slim."

Taking two steps forward, Joe pushed Hector over backwards and watched as the blood formed a pool around him. Bending forward, he picked up Hector's .45 and slid it behind his belt at the small of his back. Picking up the bloody and beaten body of Kay, he lifted her over his shoulder, wrapping his arm around her. With his own 9 mm in his left hand, he stepped over Hector before kicking the door open and walking down the hall to the rear door. He kicked the locked door open and stepped out into the night.

Chapter Nine

Joe worked his way through town. Staying in the shadows, his focus was on one thing. Seeing the sign a block away, he continued to slip from shadow to shadow. It was 2:30 in the morning and the streets were quiet.

Circling the block, he found the rear door of Alvarez Funeral Service and Crematorium. In a matter of a few seconds, Joe had the door open and walked through the business. Finding the cremation furnace, he ever so gently laid Kay's body on a cart as he figured out where everything was that he needed. He knew he needed two, possibly three, hours to cremate Kay so time was essential. Carefully, he cleaned off the rolling table. Picking up Kay's body, he placed her on it and bent over kissing her forehead, nose, and lips. Through tear-filled eyes, he slowly pushed the table inside. Pausing before he closed the door, he looked at his beautiful wife. Slowly, he pulled her out and walked back to her side. Holding her hand, his mind drifted to their first meeting, to her beautiful smile and magnificent eyes.

My god, he thought, *I absolutely loved looking into her eyes.*

He thought of climbing the mountain in Alaska and the way his heart jumped when he found her still alive. He thought about the camping trip to the Bob Marshal Wilderness Area of Montana and the way she had nursed him back to health. He thought about looking through the scope and watching in horror as Hector and five of his bottom feeding low lives had taken her. He thought about the fight and flight they felt as they ran for their lives across the deserts of Mexico. He thought about saving the women in Montana from another gang of human trafficking scum, plus the fight at Logan's ranch when Hector had tried to get her and Rene again. It was Kay and Rene that had actually saved them.

After all this time it came down to this. To just push the start button and in three hours her beautiful eyes, fantastic lips, and gorgeous smile will be nothing more than a beautiful memory.

As the tears continued to pour from his eyes, Joe West, the man who had killed terrorists, drug smugglers, and human trafficking scum, cried as he looked at a dead body. Although it wasn't just any dead body, it was the body of Kay, the woman he would have gladly died to save. The woman he had failed.

Kissing her forehead, cheeks, nose, and lips one last time, he pushed the cart inside, closing the door. He pushed the button and slowly turned and walked across the room just to drop into a chair for a terrible wait.

While waiting, Joe started to think about the smoke from the furnace chimney. Getting up, he walked to a window where he could see out while no one outside could see him. He watched as a few cars drove by. Although when a police cruiser passed slowly, he knew his time was about up.

Fifteen minutes later, the cruiser passed again. This time it stopped and checked the front door. Joe waited until the car pulled away and slipped through the building to make sure the rear door was also locked. As he waited in the shadows, he heard the rear door rattle as the officer checked the door. Giving him a few minutes to check the outside, he knew his time was up and he had to go.

Walking back into the crematorium, he shut down the furnace. It had been running for one hour and thirty minutes.

Leaving a note and 4,000 pesos, he opened the furnace. Stepping back, as the heat dissipated through the room, Joe pulled the rolling table out. He could see chunks of bone and even some unburned shards of clothing. Although he had no choice, he had to go.

Carefully, he swept Kay's ashes into a plastic container. Rearranging his backpack, he found a spot to carry her. Removing his M16, he checked the magazine and extended the stock, locking it in place. Looking through the rear window of the business, he remembered where the car was, opened the door, and stepped out into the night.

Flashing red and blue lights came on instantly. Joe's left arm swung up and tripped the trigger. He sprayed 30 supersonic 55 grain full metal jackets at the flashing lights. His first burst broke every window in a police cruiser. Second burst eliminated the flashing lights as he brought the gun to his shoulder to actually aim at his attended targets. Joe didn't want to hit the police, he just wanted to keep them pinned down while he tried to figure out a secondary plan. The car with the keys was beyond the police.

With the police not expecting a fire fight, they all ran and dove for cover, giving Joe the few seconds he needed to get around the corner of the building to temporary safety.

Seeing a car approaching, he waited until the last possible moment before stepping into the road and forcing the car to stop. Grabbing the driver's side door, he reached in and pulled the driver out. Giving him a slight push, he watched to make sure he wasn't hurt as he climbed behind the wheel. Pressing the down button for the passenger side, Joe pointed the M16 through the window as he pressed the gas pedal, hitting the cruiser in the front end, and punching several holes in the radiator. He stopped a high speed chase before it started. With the gas pedal all the way to the floor, he sped several blocks away before backing off the gas and starting to think of what to do next.

A mile away he slowed, hoping not to draw attention. Six blocks later he followed a guy into a parking lot. Parking the car, he tossed a thousand pesos and the keys on the floor, forcing the second driver from his car and leaving the parking lot. Driving cautiously, he headed west out of town hoping to get clear before daylight.

As he drove, he started looking for his cell phone to send a message to Steve and General Jacobson. Just out of town, he stopped and went through everything. Not finding the phone, he thought back. He had started to send an email when he saw the cruiser stop and started checking the doors. He remembered slipping it into his rear pocket as he headed for the back of the business.

Pausing, he thought, *It must have slipped out of my pocket in one of the cars I used. Hopefully it's actually on the ground somewhere that shouldn't draw as much attention.* Looking under the seat, he saw it. It was crushed when he forced the seat back. Picking it up, he looked at the screen and thought, *Okay, so now I have another problem. No phone and no easy way to contact Steve, General Jacobson, or to get help. Okay, now what am I going to do?*

As he sat there he heard Kay's voice, "You work better under pressure than anyone I know. You can figure this out. Just continue to do what you do best. Survive the unsurvivable."

Going through the car, he found a map. He knew very close to where he was. It was an easy decision. Panama was only a hundred miles away. Although when he ran from Medellin, he had turned and went west instead of north west. He was now about fifty miles the wrong direction. He was now in Quibdo. It would be over a hundred miles on foot through the mountains and jungles of Colombia.

Starting the engine, he saw a narrow road through the jungle headed north. Turning right, he followed the road hoping that the road would take him at least part of the way before he ran out of gas.

Three hours later, at the ground eating speed of about 20 mph, his luck ran out. The road ended in a small village on the Alralo River. Looking at the gas gauge he knew it would not get back to the Quibdo. Looking at the map again, he figured he would have a forty to sixty mile hike through the mountains and jungle to Panama. Seeing a parking lot, he parked the car. Leaving 1500 pesos and the keys under the front seat and grabbing his backpack, he walked north through the village. At the river the road ended. Joe stepped off the road and disappeared into the jungle to do what he did best. To survive the unsurvivable. He would go one on one with nature and come out on top.

Chapter Ten

Steve checked and rechecked his email several times a day for nearly two weeks when he made the decision to contact Adrian. An hour later, Adrian was sitting in Steve's office being briefed on the operation that Joe was on and the fact they hadn't heard from him in nearly two weeks. Adrian knew if Joe was alive Logan would know. Although calling wasn't an option. This had to be done face-to-face.

The following morning, he boarded a flight to Billings, Montana. He then rented a car for the several hour drive to the Rocking L. Knocking on the door, Logan looked at him and instantly knew his best friend may be dead.

 Adrian explained, "We haven't heard anything from Joe for nearly two weeks and everyone had presumed he had fallen in his quest."

Logan stumbled backwards, falling into a chair and dropping his head into his hands. The 6 foot 4 inch 265 lb ranch-hardened cowboy cried from the news.

If this information was true, then he couldn't stand the idea of Joe laying dead in a ditch somewhere or the fact that Kay was in Hector's hands. As soon as he could gather his thoughts, they called Trevor and Chance.

61

The news was overwhelming. How could Randy Jackson fail? Plans were made to get together in the next couple of days.

As they disconnected the call, Logan said, "Follow me." He headed into the office, opening his computer. He opened a file and Adrian sat down and started reading.

An hour later, Adrien asked. "Can I send this entire file to someone? Someone safe that was one of Joe's safe contacts? Someone Joe trusted completely?"

Logan replied, "Yeah, I don't see why not. If Joe is dead I want the people that are responsible to pay. I don't care if it's directly or indirectly. They just need to pay."

Adrian made a call. Steve answered on the third ring. Listening for a few minutes, he gave Adrian two email addresses. Adrian set the joint email up and, pressing send, he smiled and looked at Logan and said, "Joe is going to haunt these people from the grave for years."

At precisely 11 o'clock Eastern Time, the FBI, sheriff's department, and local police went to work, serving some 358 arrest warrants all over the country. They were disturbing court houses where the judge and lawyers were arrested. They were disturbing the house and senate in nearly every state. In Washington, Chance and several agents with Homeland Security walked into the U.S. House of Representatives, all wearing the black arm band that showed somebody from their number had made the ultimate supreme sacrifice for our country.

At the same time, Trevor was with several more agents from Homeland Security and two more squads of armory rangers walked into the Senate. They all made several arrests as senators and congressmen would finally pay for their crimes.

Adrian Sawyer along with several FBI agents walked into the White House making several more arrests.

High-ranking officials from all over the country were about to pay for the millions and millions of dollars they had made for the cocaine and heroin trade and the suffering it had caused. Plus dozens more arrested for human trafficking of women and children sold into the sex slave world where there was no escape, only pain and praying.

Joe had found enough information while in Colombia and managed to get it all sent to Adrian, Trevor, and Chance.

Two teams of Navy SEALs were dispatched to Colombia to either find, or at the worst, bring Joe West's body back to the United States.

The Colombian ambassador called the Secretary of Defense to lodge a formal complaint about a military plane flying over Columbia without prior permission. The secretary listened and said,

"I'll have to check into this and get back to you." That never happened, two minutes later the FBI walked in and he was arrested also.

In front of the federal courthouse in Washington DC, hundreds of senators, congressmen, judges, attorneys, and secretaries from the President's Cabinet were all waiting for their turn to get to a microphone and complain about the travesty being unloaded on them about them having absolutely no idea what was going on and how they were innocent of any and all charges.

As they stood there, an armored personnel carrier drove up to the crowd. As the Speaker of the House said, "I have no idea who this Randy Jackson is," in front of television cameras and nearly a hundred reporters.

The rear door opened and Randy Jackson stepped out. Handing an envelope to the Director of Homeland Security, he said, "There's enough information in here to put all of them away for many, many, years. Looking directly at the speaker of the house he said, "And that includes you."

Her mouth dropped open as she stared at the man dressed in camouflage. Her reply was crystal clear as she said directly into a live microphone, "You, you are supposed to be dead. I umm, I saw the pictures." Looking at General Jacobs, she continued, "But you, umm, you told me you had finished the job."

General Jacobs nervously looked around before saying, "I don't understand. I never said anything to you. I have no idea who this man is. I've never seen him or even a picture of him."

General Jacobson said, "The gig is up, Jacobs. We had a trace on the emails and figured out who was sending information to the House, plus someone at the FBI and Colombia." Looking over at two military MPs, he nodded. Together as one, they stepped forward, relieving General Jacobs of his side arm and taking him into custody. The MPs each had taken an arm and then stopped in front of General Jacobson.

The General shook his head in disgust and said, "I hope you enjoy Leavenworth, because that's where you are going to live for the next twenty or so years." As the MPs led Jacobs away, Special Agent Mowers walked out of the crowd. Seeing the General being led off, he looked over at the Congresswoman. With a nod of her head, he stepped forward towards General Jacobson. Joe, who was standing just behind the General, saw all of this and watched as Special Agent Mower's right hand slipped inside the left side of his suit coat. As Mower's hand came clear, Joe stepped around the General and his left fist made solid contact with Mower's jaw. As he stumbled backwards, his finger tightened on the trigger and the gun went off, grazing Joe's upper thigh. Joe's hand dropped to his thigh as he turned and stumbled into General Jacobson, pushing him out of the line of fire.

Adrain and Chance were standing just off to Joe's right. As Mower's gun discharged, both drew their weapons and fired. Mowers continued to stumble backwards as the two slugs hit him. The force of the two .40 caliber bullets lifted him off his feet and he hit the ground, bleeding from two bullet wounds, one in his upper chest and the other in his right shoulder.

The six-man team of Navy Seals and Army Special Forces flew into action and in just a few seconds they had General Jacobson and Randy Jackson pinned against the armored personnel carrier as the Seals formed a protective circle around them. As the Army Special Forces started moving, everyone backed away from the immediate area.

Other MPs rushed in to secure the area and allow emergency personnel to enter the area. Next they formed another protected ring. In ten minutes, the medical personnel got Mowers stable. Then he was transferred to the Bethesda Navy Hospital where he underwent emergency surgery.

Later he was tried for attempted murder along with several other charges.

As the commotion started to die off, General Jacobson looked at Randy, saluted, and said, "Welcome home, Commander. It's because of people like you that we enjoy the freedom this country has to offer." Then he saw the blood running down Randy's pant leg and said, "You've been shot."

Randy returned the salute as he responded, "Thank you, sir. It's just a flesh wound." Pausing, Randy looked at the crowd of reporters and continued, "Although freedom is not free. It's paid for in blood. American blood of all the military men and women who have made the ultimate sacrifice. Law enforcement officers, firefighters, and first responders. Those who run towards danger, not away from it."

Looking around once again, he continued, "Sir, it's great to be home. Although with all due respect, I just want to finish up here and go home." Turning, he looked at the small box in the back of the personal carrier. With tears running down his face, he continued, "I just want to take her home."

Two days later, Joe stumbled into his and Kay's home. Placing the beautifully carved wooden box on the coffee table, he grabbed a beer and dropped onto the couch. He had called Logan and Rene a few days before and told them he was alive, although Kay had been killed by Hector. Very possibly beaten to death. He said that he had shot Hector twice and left him to die in immense pain, that he had dropped his phone and walked over sixty miles to Panama where he had finally gotten ahold of General Jacobson. He told them that the General had sent a military jet and he was finally on his way to Washington DC. He also informed them he would be home in a few days and had a few things to do and would contact them when he was ready.

Chapter Eleven

Joe finished the beer and laid down on the couch, pulling a blanket over himself. He picked up the box containing Kay and cried himself to sleep.

Morning was cool and clear. It was a beautiful summer morning in Montana. Joe started a small fire. Then placing Kay back on the coffee table, he walked in the kitchen and made a pot of coffee. As he finished the last cup, he got up, picked up the box containing Kay and walked out to the shop. Placing her on the bench, he went to work. Several hours later he picked up Kay and went back into the house. Taking a shower, he once again laid down on the couch with Kay next to him held in a loving embrace. With tears pouring from his eyes, he drifted off.

Joe was up before daybreak. He didn't build a fire or make coffee. He walked out of the house and saddled Midnight. Putting a pack saddle on Cheyenne, he led both horses up to his shop. Dropping the reins, he walked into the house. Picking up the ornate carved box containing Kay's remains, he walked back to the shop. Placing the box into one of the packs he had put together the night before, he mounted Midnight and headed for the mountains. He watched as Midnight would sniff the pack that contained Kay. He could tell something was wrong but wasn't quite sure what it could be. Joe watched and cried as Midnight followed Cheyenne with his nose pressed against the pack. Arriving in Buffalo Valley, he set up a small camp and carried Kay to the stream-fed mountain pool where they had gone skinny dipping.

 Sitting down on the bank, he thought about making love to her right where he was currently sitting. Laughing and crying, he asked her if she remembered it. Slowly, he got up and walked back to his camp. Quickly, he built a fire and made a small supper. Putting water on, he waited and made a cup of tea. With Kay in his lap, the tears flowed from his eyes as he thought about the time they had together. He thought about the camping trip to the Bob Marshall wilderness area. He thought about saving her from the plane crash in Alaska. As he thought about their time together the tears continued until he slowly drifted off.

Joe was up before sunrise. Again, he didn't build a fire or make coffee. He walked to where the horses were tied and got them ready. After mounting Midnight, they started out. Again Midnight followed Cheyenne with his nose pressed against the pack. Joe had put the packs on the opposite side and Midnight had sniffed the one then pressed his nose against the other- the one that contained Kay's ashes. As they topped the ridge line, the valley opened up before them. Joe dismounted, dropping the reins as he went to work. Taking the large carved oak sign, he grabbed two of the large spikes he brought with it and nailed the sign to a pine tree that was located just as at the top of the ridge but before you could see the valley. Stepping back, he read, "You are entering Calamity Kay Oakley Valley, named for my loving wife who died defending what she thought was right. The traffickers got her body, heaven got her soul. I got the memories of a love I could not control. With luck and time, the love will contain the hatred that is boiling in my soul."

While standing there, Midnight walked up and hooked his head over Joe's shoulder and pulled him back a few steps. As Joe turned to pet the horse, he tucked his head under Joe's arm and covered his eyes. Joe saw and felt this. The horse now understood. The tears started again and while trying to dry his eyes, he climbed into the saddle and this time Midnight walked down the trail and stopped on the small level area they had camped several months before. Joe slid from the saddle and carefully got the carver box out of the pack. Walking to where they had slept that night months before, he pulled Kay to his chest, dropped to his knees and started crying as the tears continued flowing. He couldn't control the pain any longer. Midnight walked up behind him, sniffed the box, and dropped his head.

Two hours later, Joe got up. Getting the carved oak cross, he marked the rock wall. Then taking a battery operated drill with a diamond tipped drill bit, he drilled two holes in the rock wall. Placing two anchors in the stone, he tightened the nuts to hold the cross in place. Then with a camp shovel, he dug Kay's final resting place. She would remain here in this valley. Someday he would join her and together their ashes would remain for all eternity mixed together.

Finishing the grave, he looked to the heavens and said, "Tomorrow. I get one more night to hold you."

Looking around, Joe spotted the pile of firewood he and Kay had collected. Starting a small fire, he put coffee on and made a small meal. All the while he talked to Kay. About their trip together into this valley, about the two elk mounts he had gotten back, aout putting them above the fireplace. As day turned to night, he slid into a sleeping bag, balled up his jacket and pulled Kay next to him under the covers. With her in his arms, he slowly drifted off.

Joe's eyes opened before the sun started to rise in the eastern sky. He could see the horses just a few feet away. Midnight walked up and sniffed at the wooden box, dropping his head so Joe could scratch him between the ears. As Joe started to get dressed, Midnight stood there like he was standing guard, ears up and alert. Joe got a watertight plastic box and placed Kay in it. Taking it to the grave, he had dug the afternoon before. He slowly and gently placed her in her final resting place. Stopping, he dropped a pin to Logan's phone and then quickly sent a text.

A few minutes later Logan's reply came through only two words: **Got it.**

Joe sat there knowing he couldn't do what he had to do next. Pouring a cup of coffee, he sat there and again the tears came. An hour later, he had finally finished. Pouring another cup, he moved closer and sat there staring at Calamity Kay Oakley Valley. As he looked at the valley, Midnight once again walked across the small clearing and stood over him. Getting up, he scratched him between the ears and walked away to fill his coffee cup. Turning, he watched as Midnight slowly and carefully laid down next to Kay's grave. As Joe watched Midnight, the tears started to flow again. Joe walked over and sat down next to the beautiful black horse. Laying his head against the horse's front shoulder, Joe let it all out. All the pain he had been holding in came out. He reached his arms around the horse's neck and cried. He couldn't hold back and he couldn't stop. Nothing else mattered at that point in time. It had to come out.

Joe laid there against Midnight. Closing his eyes, he thought about the flight he and Logan had made to look and eventually purchase the beautiful black Arabian stallion for Kay. Joe fondly remembered the look on her face when she finally realized he was hers, how happy and thankful Kay was that night. This brought a momentary smile to his face and through the tears he let out a short chuckle.

Getting up, he threw a saddle on Cheyenne and looked at Midnight. "Come on, boy. Let's go home."

Swinging into the saddle, he watched as Midnight got up and followed. Stopping every few feet and looking back, Joe stopped and waited for him to catch up.

Reaching over, he patted his neck and said, "You can come up here whenever you want to visit her and I'll come with you."

Turning, he started the six hour ride home. As he rode he continued to think about Kay and their life together. Smiling, he recalled meeting her for the first time. The way he watched as she moved through the room. The way he worked his way trying to get close to her. The butterflies that invaded his system as their hands touched. Putting his number in her hand as he had left the party. Waiting and praying she would call. Scared she would and scared she wouldn't. Meeting her at the coffee and ice cream shop. Her beautiful smile and those amazing eyes. About the second time they went out. What a beautiful evening. A fantastic meal and several hours walking and talking as they strolled along the beach.

Finally getting home, he removed the saddle from Cheyenne and turned both horses into the pasture. Looking at the house, he knew he had to go inside although he really didn't want to. Taking a deep breath, he opened the door and slowly walked inside. Grabbing a beer, he dropped onto the couch and continued to wipe the tears as the thoughts of Kay refused to leave his mind. As the hours passed, he finally closed his eyes to a night filled with dreams and nightmares. He dreamt about the horror of finding Kay's beaten and bloody body in Tunja, about trying over and over again to find a heartbeat or any kind of sign that she was still alive. He thought about finally realizing he had been too late to save her and he had failed on his promise to always protect her. He thought about shooting Hector twice and the satisfaction that gave him. He thought about the six day walk through the jungle carrying her, trying to get to Panama and not knowing what would happen when he got there.

Chapter Twelve

Two thousand miles away, a military Cessna Citation taxied towards the active runway at Joint Base Andrews Naval Air Facility in Washington DC. At the controls sat Captain Alex Esperanza and Lieutenant Jane Rodrigues. At precisely 8:00 am, the Military Citation pilots pushed the throttles full forward as the jet gained speed and lifted off into the storm filled skies and climbed to its cruising altitude of 41,000 feet.

Precisely one hour later, a six man squad of Army Rangers left from the Joint Base Lewis McCord near Tacoma Washington for a two hour flight to Billings, Montana. Arriving an hour early, they secured the area for inbound VIP.

As Cessna Citation landed, the Army Rangers formed a protective area encircling the VIP and escorted them to the waiting motorcade for the two hour drive to their final destination.

Logan sat drinking his morning coffee and watched as the motorcade pulled up and stopped in front of his house. Walking out onto the deck, he watched as General Jacobson got out of the car followed by three Army Rangers and slowly walked up the stairs.

Shaking hands with General Jacobson, he asked, "Are you ready?"

Logan replied, "No, but yes."

General Jacobson motioned for Logan to follow him. After a short conversation, Logan looked at General Jacobson and said, "Are you sure? I mean, you're kidding right?"

To which the general replied, "Nope, I'm serious."

Logan walked to the table and scribbled a quick note. Then looking at the gentsays, he said, "I had better be towards the front of the line when we get to Joe's. He's been a little jumpy lately and I don't want him to shoot anyone."

Joe was instantly on his feet as he heard the vehicles pull into his driveway. Looking out the window, he swore as he quickly walked into his gun room and grabbed a pistol.

Logan walked up to the door followed by Trevor, Chance, Adrain, General Jacobson, and Sargent Colton and knocked on Joe's front door. As Joe answered the door, he looked from one to another before he said, "What did I do to receive such an early morning honor like this?"

With that, Logan stepped aside as did Trevor, Chance, Sargent Colton, General Jacobson, Captain Esperanza, and Lieutenant Rodriguez. Then from behind the huge muscular body of Adrian Sawyer stepped a beautiful black haired lady with the most beautiful eyes Joe had ever seen.

Joe took only two steps before his legs buckled and he dropped to his knees as Kay ran forward trying to catch him. General Jacobson and Sargent Colton caught Joe, trying to keep him on his feet as everyone moved forward trying to get to him. Joe turned and once again looked into the amazing eyes of Kay, fighting to get free from the grip of the men holding him. In three steps, he had his arms wrapped around her. He couldn't control it. The tears and sobs started as he rocked back and forth holding his wife.

For the next nearly thirty minutes, no one said a word as they both refused to let go of the other. Kissing ,crying, and hugging each other. Joe ran his thumbs across Kay's eyes. Clearing the tears away again and again. He couldn't believe he was actually holding her again. Kay just held on. Refusing to let go. She could feel the anger and tension drain away as it left his body and the loving tender man she had fallen in love with returned to her.

Just a mile away, Rene returned home from shopping. Carrying in the first load of groceries, she saw Logan's note on the kitchen table. As she read it, the tears started to flow. She couldn't believe it. Kay was alive and home. In a matter of minutes, she was out the door and headed for the West home. Pulling into the driveway, Rene left the pickup running and the door open.

She ran towards the house screaming, "Kay! Kay! Oh my god you're alive!" Bursting through the door, she nearly tackled Kay.

One of the Rangers was only a step behind her as Logan stepped into his path and said, "It's okay, she's my wife and Kay's best friend."

Quickly, the Ranger glanced at General Jacobson who nodded and said, "Stand down corporal. She is safe." With that, the corporal did a about face. He marched outside to park the pickup and shut off the engine.

As everyone started to settle down, Kay started to tell her story. Hector had hit her so hard he knocked her unconscious. She came too in a room with a dead body. Then Kay realized the lady was nearly the same size as her, with black hair and a slightly darker complexion. As quickly as possible, she changed clothes with the lady, finding her identification and getting the window open.

She realized she had taken her ring with the transmitter in it and left it on the nightstand next to the bed. She had panicked when she heard the door rattle as she realized she needed the ring. However she didn't have time, so she slipped out the window and ran, too afraid to look back for fear someone was chasing her.

She ran and saw a Catholic Church. Remembering the church in the small village where she was taken at gunpoint the first time by Hector, she prayed the priest would speak English. Finding the priest, she told him she was running from Hector and needed help. He had hidden her for two days while Hector's men had nearly torn the town apart trying to find her.

They had snuck her out in the middle of the night and began the twenty mile walk to Bogota. After two days, she had finally convinced them to check. The only person she could remember was Oliver Scott. It was only after they had finally contacted him in Springfield and confirmed that Randy Jackson was actually an agent and that he was currently running an operation in Colombia. He was trying to find his granddaughter that had been kidnapped by a human trafficking organization and hopefully also get his wife back who had traded herself knowing that there was a very strong possibility that she would probably end up being sold into the sex slave world anyway.

Joe looked shocked at that information and the fact that he owed Oliver an apology, plus a huge thank you for telling the truth about something after all the bad blood between them.

As Kay talked, Rene started cooking and Logan fired up the grill. It was steak for everyone. Sargent Colton had to walk out to tell the Rangers to come in and eat. Lieutenant Alex Jeffries refused, although they would eat only if they could remain outside and not abandon their position. It was only after General Jacobson gave them a direct order telling them to stand down that they actually sat down to eat. Rene carried plates containing ribeye steaks, baked potatoes, green beans, and corn and their choice of what to drink. Each and everyone of the rangers refused to leave their position although they did enjoy a fantastic meal. After General Jacobson gave them a second direct order, the Rangers came inside to meet the legendary Randy Jackson. They all knew who he was and it was an honor to meet him and stand as bodyguards to protect and witness the return of Kay.

Joe walked to the window and, looking out, he thought about how Midnight had acted as they brought what he had thought was Kay's ashes up into the mountains and finally into the valley.

Turning to Logan, Joe motioned for him to follow. As they walked away from the others, he explained how Midnight had acted, reminding him of the fact it wasn't Kay's remains in the box.

Logan smiled as he replied, "You told me there was unburnt clothing mixed in with the ashes. That clothing actually belonged to Kay. Midnight could smell Kay. He didn't care about what else he could smell. He only cared about Kay and the fact he could smell her but not find her."

Looking back at Kay, he said, "Honey, come here." He opened the sliding glass doors and walked out onto the deck. Kay walked up beside him, slipping her hand into his. Midnight's head came up, his nostrils flared and he whinnied.

Logan heard the horse and carefully got everyone's attention. He had never in all the years he had been around horses heard a whinny like that. Watching out the windows, everyone witnessed just how much an animal could love a human. Midnight made one half circle around the corral and sailed over the six foot fence as he raced across the ranch yard just to the sliding stop directly in front of Kay with Joe standing behind her.

Taking his head, he reached over Kay's shoulder and pulled her towards him, like he was trying to hug her. He continued to step back and forth, then circle both, until Joe started scratching him between the ears. Slowly, he started to calm down. Joe put his hands like a stirrup and lifted Kay onto his back. Midnight started prancing around the ranch yard and turning, he stopped in front of Joe. Kay threw her leg over his neck and Joe caught her as she slid to the ground. Midnight watched as Kay walked to stand next to Joe.

Using his nose, Midnight pushed Kay in front of Joe. Then reaching over them both, he hooked his chin on Joe's shoulder and pulled them both against his chest. He finally understood she belonged to him. Although they were both his.

Epilogue

Four thousand miles away in Medellin, Colombia, Juan and Pablo watched as Hector slept, fighting for his life. The surgeon had done everything possible now and it was up to Hector and God.

Juan said, "I'm going to the US and kill Joe West if possible, that damn cowboy Logan Lathrop also. But Joe is definitely going to die."

At the other end of the building, the leaders of the Colombian cartel were in a closed door meeting talking about what had just happened and the fact that they had lost all their contacts and protection in the US due to one man.

Luis Costello stood up and said, "Who is this man? Does anyone know where he came from?"

Mario Sanches replied, "He's like the ghost. The Ghost of Colombia from years ago."

Luis slammed his fist on the table and screamed, "Ghost, my ass! He's just a man. A man I want dead. This time we do it my way. Get Juan and Pablo in here. They'll follow my orders or they'll be laying next to Hector only all three will be dead! And Snaches contact our friends in Los Angeles. It's time we bring MS into this. They are in the United States and that's their territory. They can fix it. Fix it my way and my way only!"

To be continued…